FLOWER SHOP ON MAGNOLIA

BLUE HERON COTTAGES
BOOK SIX

KAY CORRELL

ZURA LU PUBLISHING LLC

This book is dedicated to yellow roses. Strange, I know. But yellow was my mother's favorite color. I can't help but smile and remember her when I see yellow roses. Or yellow anything. I miss you, Mom.

Fate brought them together. But will Daisy's promises keep them apart?

Daisy's new flower shop in Moonbeam has a nice steady flow of customers. But it's so different from back home in Colorado.

No, Colorado was not home. Not anymore. She can never return. Not after what happened.

Jack moves to Moonbeam to help take care of his mother, though his mom insists she doesn't need help. Okay, so maybe he just needs a change and used his mom as an excuse. But what he really needs is to find a place to live.

Luckily, Daisy's neighbor needs a renter and Jack ends up living next door to Daisy. What starts as a friendship quickly blossoms into something more.

But Daisy made two promises to

herself. Promise one: swearing off having a relationship. But her heart tells her it might be okay to take a chance with Jack. Maybe

Then disaster strikes. Even if she would consider breaking the first promise, she will not break the second one. She can't. And a relationship with Jack would shatter that promise into tiny grains of sand.

But Moonbeam has a way of weaving its charm through the lives of the people in town. One never knows what may happen...

KAY'S BOOKS

Find more information on all my books at
kaycorrell.com
Buy direct from Kay's Shop at
shop.kaycorrell.com

COMFORT CROSSING ~ THE SERIES

The Wedding in the Grove - (a crossover short story between series - with Josephine and Paul from The Letter.)

LIGHTHOUSE POINT ~ THE SERIES

Wish Upon a Shell - Book One
Wedding on the Beach - Book Two
Love at the Lighthouse - Book Three
Cottage near the Point - Book Four
Return to the Island - Book Five
Bungalow by the Bay - Book Six
Christmas Comes to Lighthouse Point - Book Seven

CHARMING INN ~ Return to Lighthouse Point

One Simple Wish - Book One
Two of a Kind - Book Two
Three Little Things - Book Three
Four Short Weeks - Book Four
Five Years or So - Book Five
Six Hours Away - Book Six
Charming Christmas - Book Seven

SWEET RIVER ~ THE SERIES

A Dream to Believe in - Book One

A Memory to Cherish - Book Two

A Song to Remember - Book Three

A Time to Forgive - Book Four

A Summer of Secrets - Book Five

A Moment in the Moonlight - Book Six

MOONBEAM BAY ~ THE SERIES

The Parker Women - Book One

The Parker Cafe - Book Two

A Heather Parker Original - Book Three

The Parker Family Secret - Book Four

Grace Parker's Peach Pie - Book Five

The Perks of Being a Parker - Book Six

BLUE HERON COTTAGES ~ THE SERIES

Memories of the Beach - Book One

Walks along the Shore - Book Two

Bookshop near the Coast - Book Three

Restaurant on the Wharf - Book Four

Lilacs by the Sea - Book Five

Flower Shop on Magnolia - Book Six

More to come!

WIND CHIME BEACH ~ A stand-alone novel

INDIGO BAY ~

Sweet Days by the Bay - Kay's Complete
Collection of stories in the Indigo Bay series

Sign up for my newsletter at my website
kaycorrell.com to make sure you don't miss any
new releases or sales.

CHAPTER 1

The door to Beach Blooms flew open just before closing time, startling Daisy, and she dropped her scissors with a clatter. She looked up from her workbench where she was arranging a simple bouquet in a mason jar as a man stepped inside.

He ran his gaze around the shop, looking a bit panicked, and quickly crossed the distance to her. "Afternoon, ma'am. Glad you're open. I'm looking for flowers."

"You've come to the right place." She glanced around at all the flowers on display in her shop, suppressing a smile.

"Right. I mean… I need a bouquet. No, not that. A pin-on thingie."

"A pin-on thingie?"

"You know, a thing of flowers you pin on a woman." He shrugged and gave her a lopsided grin.

"A corsage?"

He snapped his fingers. "Yes, that's it." His brown eyes glittered with relief.

"Okay, when do you need it?"

"I need it right now. Well, it's for tomorrow morning. But, you know, I'd need to get it now."

"Ah, okay. I can make you one. Do you know what kind of flowers you want?"

He frowned and chewed his bottom lip. "No. I don't. She likes yellow, though. That's her favorite color."

"Okay, I have some yellow roses. I could do a rose with some baby's breath and a bit of greenery."

"Sure. I mean, I guess." He let out a long breath. "My brother usually orders this, but he's gone. He could have at least left me some instructions. Told me what he usually does. Now I'm here and I'm left to do this. I better not screw it up."

"Okay…" She wasn't quite sure who or

what she was making the corsage for, but the customer was always right.

"But no, that sounds great. Anything."

So he wasn't a really picky customer. Some people were like that about flowers, but she'd never understand that attitude. She reached into the fridge, pulled out a single yellow rose, and started to make the corsage.

It was a bit of a strange request. One corsage. Didn't sound like it was for a wedding, and he was way past the prom age. She glanced at him, then back at her work. He looked to be about her age, actually. A dark tan that spoke of a life in the sun. Muscular arms stretched out of a faded, worn gray t-shirt. A few strands of gray peeked out at his temples.

He looked over her shoulder. "I really appreciate this. My brother would never let me live it down if I didn't to get this. That looks really nice."

She finished up the corsage and boxed it in a clear container. "You'll need to keep it refrigerated until you give it to her. I hope she likes it."

"Me, too. I'm sure she will."

She led him over to the checkout, rang him

KAY CORRELL

up, and he paid for the purchase. She glanced at the name on the charge. Jackson Rayburn.

He picked up the box. "Thanks. I was really glad to see you were still open. I almost wrecked everything."

"Glad I could help."

He flashed her a smile, then turned and strode across the shop in a few quick steps. He stopped in front of the door and turned back around. "Oh, and nice shop you have here. Super glad you're here in Moonbeam, so I didn't have to go driving all over searching for a flower shop. Anyway, thank you. Oh, and I didn't catch your name."

"Daisy."

He grinned. "Great name for a florist." With that, he slipped out the door.

She shook her head. She'd heard that before. Daisy didn't know if she became a florist because of her name or if the universe had nudged her mother into naming her Daisy because it knew that all things flowers would be her calling in life. Either way, she was glad to have her flower shop here in Moonbeam. Glad that she'd recently found a new place to live. A place far from

Colorado. A state she vowed she'd never return to.

But she'd found Moonbeam, a quaint beach town on the southwest coast of Florida, and she loved it so far. She didn't have many friends yet. Okay, really had none. But she was slowly getting to know people. The townsfolk were friendly, and business had slowly begun to blossom. She smiled at her thoughts. She even thought in terms of flowers.

She finished the bouquet she'd been arranging in the mason jar and plopped it into the refrigerated display. Then she adjusted the container of yellow roses that didn't look quite right since she'd snagged one for the corsage. She wasn't certain what woman was getting a corsage for what reason, but she'd done her job. She went over and flipped the sign on the door to closed, then wandered around straightening and putting some more flowers back into the refrigerated display case. She stood back and surveyed her handiwork. The shop was coming together nicely in the few weeks she'd been open. She loved her work, loved owning Beach Blooms. Loved being away from Colorado…

She turned out the lights and slipped out the

door, locking it behind her. It was a short walk to her cottage on the beach, and she enjoyed her leisurely strolls home after her days in the shop. And it was nice to not have to bundle up against Colorado's bitter cold. She shoved those thoughts away.

Florida. Moonbeam. A new start on life. Things would be much better here. They had to be.

Jack ducked into his cottage at Blue Heron Cottages and placed the corsage in the refrigerator as instructed. At least he hadn't screwed that up. Tomorrow was his mother's birthday, and he'd just found out his brother, Shane, always ordered her a corsage to wear to church for the Sunday nearest her birthday. Evidently, the churchgoers would all ooh and ahh over it and wish her a happy birthday. Fine. If that was some kind of tradition, he could run with it. At least he could now that he had the corsage. Anyway, he didn't want to disappoint his mother.

Well, not more than he already had by

staying at the cottages instead of with her. He just couldn't see himself sleeping on her pull-out couch. He'd been looking for a place to live since he moved here to Moonbeam, but it had only been a month or so. First, he'd stayed at The Cabot Hotel, but that was pricey, and he really wanted to be on the beach. He'd found Blue Heron Cottages a few days ago and moved in here.

He dropped into a chair by the brightly painted table—this Violet woman who owned the cottages sure liked bright colors—and snapped open his laptop, searching for any new listing. A cottage directly on the beach would be ideal, but so far he'd had no luck. Not that he'd had much time to look. Between his job working remotely for his company and his weekend gig, he barely had time to breathe.

And things had happened too quickly. His brother got a job offer that he said he couldn't refuse. Great money, good promotion. And he up and moved to San Diego. But neither of them thought it was a good idea for their mother to live here in Moonbeam without any family around. Since Jack could work remotely, it only made sense that he move here. Besides, as Shane had told him at least a million times, his brother had been here with their mother for years. It was Jack's time to step up.

Not that he disagreed. Shane *had* lived here in Moonbeam for years, and the new job *was* a great opportunity for him. Besides, Jack didn't really mind moving here. It was a nice enough town. It was just that he hadn't exactly had a choice. He liked choices.

But his mother was so happy. Even with all her protests that he didn't have to move here. That she'd be fine living here alone. His mom and dad had moved here for retirement, but then their dad passed away suddenly. Shane had moved down here and found a job in nearby Sarasota. Now he was gone off to San Diego. Shane had probably done a much better job than he was doing with everything. He'd almost forgotten tomorrow was his mother's birthday. Luckily, Shane had texted to remind him. And mentioned the whole corsage thing. Had his brother expected him to just know a little detail like that?

He shut the lid on his computer. No new listings. It was going to get pretty pricey staying months at hotels and the cottages. But there was no way he was sleeping on that pull-out couch.

He really needed to find a place. Something had to turn up. He wasn't eager to go back to apartment living, but he might have to. He had looked at one apartment complex. It was crammed full of twentysomething kids. Not exactly his style.

He glanced at his watch. He still had time to get in a quick run on the beach before sunset. That would clear his mind. Something so peaceful about running along the water's edge. Besides, he needed to keep in shape.

He got into his running clothes and headed out to the beach, sure the run would soothe his nerves.

CHAPTER 2

Daisy sat out on the porch of her cottage, relaxing and watching the sunset unfold. She loved this time of day. A breeze blew in from off the water. Waves rolled to the shore in what should be a steady, soothing motion. As if anything could truly soothe her these days.

She sucked in a deep breath of the salty air, so different from the crisp, piney air in Colorado. But Colorado was behind her now. Florida was where she lived. It was where she'd decided to pick up and move her shop. Even though she'd had to learn a lot about what flowers and plants grew down here in Florida and which were easy to source versus back home.

No, Colorado was *not* home.

She stood up and walked over to the railing, chasing away the unease she felt anytime she thought about Colorado. Which was, unfortunately, often. She'd hoped by now that she'd feel like Moonbeam was home. But she still felt like a stranger, even though everyone had been so welcoming to her. Told her how happy they were to finally have a florist in Moonbeam.

But she couldn't help but feel a small nagging that she was just running away. Hiding. But that wasn't it—it wasn't. She just needed this fresh start.

A lone man came running up the beach, and she recognized him as the guy who bought the corsage. She lifted a hand in a wave, and he slowed his pace and jogged up to her cottage. He bent his tall frame over for a moment, catching his breath before standing back up. His damp t-shirt stretched across his chest, and his face was red from the exertion or maybe the breeze.

"Hello there, Daisy."

"Hi, Jackson."

He raised an eyebrow. "You know my name?"

She smiled. "From the receipt. And I'm good at remembering names."

"Ah, of course. Well, my mother calls me Jackson, and so does the IRS, but everyone else calls me Jack."

"Duly noted."

He stood on the sand, still catching his breath.

"Would you like some water?"

"I would."

She went inside, got a large glass of ice water, and brought it out to him. He finished it in a few quick gulps. "Thank you."

"More?"

"Nah, I'm good."

"Do you live around here?" She couldn't remember seeing him on the beach before.

"I'm staying at Blue Heron Cottages. I've been here in Moonbeam for a little over a month or so. I've actually been looking for a place to rent, but haven't had much luck."

"Oh, my neighbor is putting his house up for rent. He's moving up north by his kids but doesn't really want to sell in case he doesn't like living up there. He said he's going to give it a year's try and then decide. You could talk to him."

"Really? That would be great."

"Come on, let's go see if he's home." She led the way to the cottage next to hers and rapped on the door.

Mr. Cooper opened the door. "Hi, Daisy."

"Hi, Mr. Cooper. This is Jack. He's looking for a place to rent. I know you said you were going to rent your place." She looked past him at stacks of packed boxes.

"I am. I was just getting ready to list it. Guess I should have done that sooner since I'm almost packed. Going to head up this week with my things. I'm planning on renting the place furnished."

Jack reached out and shook Mr. Cooper's hand. "I'm Jack Rayburn. Nice to meet you."

"Are you Mona Rayburn's son?"

Jack nodded. "I am."

She glanced at Jack. His mother lived here in Moonbeam? Wonder why he wasn't staying with her.

"Heard you'd come to town, and that Shane

had moved away. Though Mona insisted you didn't need to move here. That she'd been fine."

"So I've heard," Jack said wryly.

"Being Mona's son is a great reference for a renter." Mr. Cooper grinned.

"I'll let you two talk and see if you can work it out." Daisy turned away and headed back to her cottage to let the men figure out the details.

Of course Mr. Cooper knew Jack's mother. It seemed like everyone knew everyone here in Moonbeam. Not that it was that different back home in Sweet River Falls.

Colorado was not home, she reminded herself. Again.

She shook her head. Would she ever stop thinking about that place? She went inside long enough to grab a beer, then settled down on a chair to watch what was left of the sunset.

After a while, Jack came back over and climbed the stairs to the porch. "Daisy, I can't thank you enough. First you saved me with my mother's birthday corsage for her to wear to church tomorrow. Now you found me a place to rent right on the beach. Reasonable rent too. He mentioned some things that needed repair around the place and I said I'd fix them for him."

His mother. The corsage was a birthday corsage for his *mother*.

"I'm glad it worked out."

He nodded at her beer. "Don't suppose you'd have another one of those?"

"Of course." She jumped up and went inside and grabbed one for him. She returned and handed the icy bottle to him, and he took a long swig. "Ah, thanks. Just what I needed. I haven't had time to really stock my kitchen at Blue Heron Cottages. Now it looks like I'll be stocking the cottage next door. He's leaving midweek."

"Really?"

"Yep, so it looks like on Wednesday I'll be your new neighbor." He flashed an impish grin. "I'm a pretty great neighbor."

"You don't say." She grinned back at him. That didn't sound so bad. Having Jack as a neighbor. He certainly was friendly. And he said he was handy, which would be nice if anything broke. And he'd gotten flowers for his mother for her birthday. How could she not like a man who did that?

"You want to sit a bit? We can watch the rest of the sunset."

He sank onto the metal chair beside her. "Don't mind if I do. I enjoy watching the sun set over the ocean. Well, the Gulf, I guess."

"I always just think of it as the ocean, even if people like to correct me."

"Then we're in agreement. Ocean it is." He took another swallow of beer.

It was enjoyable sitting here having an easy conversation with Jack. She'd missed that. Just sitting and chatting with friends. Maybe Jack could be her first friend here in Moonbeam.

He rose from his chair. "Thanks for the drink. I better go hit the shower. But at least I can take looking for a place to live off of my list. Appreciate that."

"Glad to help."

He climbed down the stairs and paused. "I guess I'll be seeing you around."

"I guess you will."

He gave a little wave of his hand and jogged off toward Blue Heron Cottages. She picked up their empty bottles and headed inside, pulling the French door closed behind her. The silence of the cottage loomed around her as she padded across the floor. She flipped on some lights and headed to the kitchen. After making a sandwich, she stood at the sink eating it, the epitome of a lonely single woman. She rinsed the dish and set it in the dishwasher, assuring herself that change was hard, and she'd soon get used to her new life. Although she'd been telling herself that for over a year now. First throughout her travels, then after finding Moonbeam and settling down here. Her new *home*.

CHAPTER 3

J ack got up early the next morning and sat out on the porch, sipping his coffee. Relief flowed through him at finally finding a place to rent. That should keep his mother from constantly insisting he come stay with her.

Soon he'd have a place of his own. Living out of hotels made him antsy, unsettled. At least here at Blue Heron Cottages he had a kitchen. Not that he'd used it for anything but making coffee so far. And he was extremely tired of eating at restaurants or munching on takeout.

He took out his phone and started a list of groceries to buy for his new place. What a bonus to find a place being rented out completely furnished. One less thing to worry about. He glanced at his watch. Better gulp this coffee down and run by his mother's place so she'd have the corsage for church this morning.

He finished the coffee, grabbed the corsage from the fridge, and debated between driving or walking. He was cutting it close, though, so he took his car.

A short time later he pulled into the drive at his mother's villa. She lived in a nice little retirement area filled with attached villas. A monthly fee covered the maintenance, so she didn't have to worry about the yard and had a service to call for repairs. It was a safe little place, too. He liked that.

She probably would have been fine here alone, but really, he could live anywhere, so there was no reason not to move here and keep an eye on her. Be here to help her with anything she needed. Check in on her now and then. Okay, and she was a world-class cook. There was that. He had to run extra miles to keep off the pounds from all the big meals she'd cooked for him since he'd arrived.

He sprang up the steps and knocked on the door.

"Come in," his mother called out.

He pushed inside. "Mom?"

"Back in the kitchen."

He hurried to the kitchen, then pulled out the flowers from behind his back with a flourish. "Happy birthday, Mom."

"Oh, a corsage. Thank you." She reached for it, beaming with a smile from ear to ear. "I didn't know if I'd have one this year since Shane moved."

"Hey, I'm here. Of course you got one this year." When he'd finally been told at the last minute to get one.

She crossed over to a mirror and pinned it on. "Doesn't that look nice? And yellow. My favorite. Thank you, Jackson."

"You're welcome. Are we still on for a birthday dinner tonight on the wharf?"

"I told you I could cook for us."

"Mom, it's your birthday. You don't need to cook a meal for us on your birthday."

"But I wouldn't mind."

"Nope, we're going out. Oh, and guess what? I found a cottage to rent. Not too far from here. It's right near Blue Heron Cottages. Mr. Cooper's place."

"Oh, he's such a nice man. I hope he enjoys living up north by his kids and grandkids."

"I'm pretty sure I got the place because you're my mom." He winked at her. "Thanks for that."

"Glad to help." When she smiled, the lines beside her eyes deepened. When had she gotten this old? In his mind, he still pictured her with boundless energy, brown hair—not totally gray—and not a wrinkle to be found. But here she was. The same, just older. Of course, when he looked in the mirror, it shocked him to see the strands of gray in his own hair.

"Want me to drop you off at church? I'm headed out for a fill-in shift."

"I'll walk. It only takes me a few minutes."

He kissed her cheek. "Okay. I'll pick you up at six for dinner?"

"Six will be fine."

He knew she really preferred to eat earlier than that, but he would be pushing it to finish work, grab a shower, and get back here by six. "Okay. See you then." He headed out to his car, ready for a day out in the fresh air. He liked his day job and that he could work remotely, but this side job where he was out in the sunshine was perfect. Didn't pay much, but he loved it. Besides, it kept him busy. He wasn't one to sit around much. Hadn't made many friends here in Moonbeam yet, either.

Well, maybe one. His new neighbor, Daisy.

Melody had been up since five a.m. She'd baked a loaf of bread to use for sandwiches. Then a cake. She had the picnic lunch all planned out for her date with Ethan today. Her *second* date with Ethan. Butterflies fluttered around in her stomach. Hadn't she firmly decided that she wasn't nervous about dating Ethan? How come the butterflies didn't listen to her?

But now the hours until Ethan was picking her up for their picnic stretched out before her. Maybe she'd go visit Violet at Blue Heron Cottages. Violet and Rose usually had coffee each morning. She'd join them.

Great idea. She congratulated herself on figuring out something that would at least kill an hour or so. She couldn't just stay here baking all day. She already had way too much food for the picnic.

As expected, Violet was sitting out on the front porch with Rose. "Morning." She climbed the stairs.

"Morning, Melody. Coffee's inside on the counter if you want some." Violet nodded toward the office.

"Perfect." She went in, grabbed a cup, and came out to sit beside them.

"Just out for an early walk?" Rose asked.

"I'm trying to kill time. I've already baked enough for twenty picnic baskets."

"Oh, for your date with Ethan?" Violet asked.

"Yes. That one. I hope he's hungry." She laughed.

"Where are you going for your picnic?" Rose tilted her head to the side, a small smile resting on her lips.

"I'm not sure. The beach somewhere, I guess. Or maybe the gazebo in the town park? Guess I should figure that out."

"Or Ethan will," Rose said, her eyes twinkling.

"Right, I forget I don't have to plan every little thing. Okay, I did plan every little thing for the picnic basket. Way overplanned.

24

Overbought. Overbaked. But it kept me busy while I couldn't sleep."

"You'll probably get used to going on dates after a bit." Violet's lips tipped up in amusement.

"You think? I don't know." She shook her head. "It still seems strange."

"But you had a good time when you went to dinner at The Cabot Hotel, didn't you?" Rose leaned forward in her chair.

"I did."

"The Jenkins twins have been spreading the news all over town that you two had that date." Violet laughed.

"I know. Everyone who comes into Sea Glass Cafe while I'm working asks me about it." She shook her head. "Those two just love to spread gossip around town.

"I think they were genuinely happy for you, though." Violet stood. "More coffee, anyone?"

"Sure." Rose held out her cup.

"I'm fine." She stared into her cup. She didn't really need more coffee. She'd had multiple cups this morning, and the caffeine would only add to her jitters. She set the cup down on the table next to her.

Violet came out and settled into her chair again. "There's a chance for showers this afternoon. I hope they don't ruin your picnic."

"Oh, I hadn't even checked the weather. I hope it doesn't rain." Then what would they do? She needed a backup plan.

Violet laughed. "I can almost hear your mind working."

"It pays to be prepared." She wasn't one for surprises.

Rose blew on her coffee, then took a sip. "Maybe you should just let the day unfold as it's intended."

That was easier said than done.

"Did you figure out what you're going to wear?" Violet asked, then laughed. "I know that's a problem for you."

"Just shorts and a t-shirt, I think. Nothing fancy." She frowned. "Right? That's what you wear to a picnic?"

"I'm sure anything you wear will be fine," Rose assured her.

She bit her lip. Maybe she should wear a sundress? Since it was an official date? But sitting on a picnic blanket in a dress wasn't the best idea she'd ever had.

"Wear one of those cute new tops we got you when we went shopping last week. They'll be fine," Violet suggested. "That with shorts or capris will work."

"You're right. I'm just overthinking everything. Let's talk about something else."

"We can talk about Rose saying she might actually leave soon and go back home." Violet frowned. "I'm not pleased."

"I do have to go home sometime. I can't stay here forever."

"I think you could." Violet countered. "I've loved having you here. You're my friend now. I'll miss you."

"I haven't decided for sure when I'll leave yet."

"Good, then maybe I can convince you to stay a lot longer."

"I do have things to deal with back home." Rose sighed. "But I'm still not sure I'm ready to deal with them. To make some hard decisions I have to make."

"What better place to procrastinate on making decisions than here in Moonbeam?" Melody glanced at her cup, wondering if she should pick it up and finish it. No, she shouldn't.

"You're right about that. No better place." Rose bobbed her head. "I've had a wonderful time here. I love the cottages and everything Violet has done to them."

This had been a great idea to come visit with Rose and Violet. She glanced at her watch. Oh, lovely. She'd just killed *thirty-five* minutes. It was going to be a long morning.

CHAPTER 4

Annoyed at her indecisiveness, Melody finally slipped on an outfit for her date. The picnic basket was packed and ready. She'd found an old blanket they could use on the beach.

If they were going to the beach…

Was she this nervous when she first dated her husband, John? She couldn't really remember. It bothered her that a lot of her memories with John had dimmed a bit. Maybe it was her mind's way of protecting her heart from the pain of losing him. She glanced over at the dresser to a photo of them. They'd been out for dinner on the wharf. John was laughing, and her hair was blowing crazily about her face.

But they both looked so happy. And they were, up until John got so sick. "Hope you're okay with this, John. Know that I still love you."

She shook her head. Was it only a crazy woman who talked to a photo like this? She spun on her heels and headed to the kitchen to check the picnic basket for like the hundredth time.

The clock on the wall ticked away the seconds ever so slowly. Would it ever be time for Ethan to get here? A knock at the door sounded, and she glanced at the clock again. Twenty minutes early?

She hurried over and opened the door. Ethan stood there grinning. "I know I'm early. This was the longest morning in history. I couldn't wait any longer. But if you're not ready, I'll just sit out here on the step until you are."

She laughed and pulled him inside. "You could have come a half hour ago, and I'd have been ready." He could have come an hour early and she would've been ready—except for the whole choosing an outfit thing.

She led the way to the kitchen. "Here's the picnic... with way too much food. And I got a blanket because I wasn't sure where we're going."

"Is the beach okay? I thought we'd go to the one near my house. I have a beach wagon ready, along with a blanket, an umbrella, and a cooler of soda and water."

"You are prepared." She handed him the basket, and they went out to his car. He held the door open for her and she slid inside. A ripple of nerves raced through her. Okay, here she was. Starting her second date with Ethan. The butterflies flitted again.

He drove them back to his house and loaded up the wagon. He pulled it down the short walkway to the beach, and they found a place near the water's edge.

She glanced up at the sky as the clouds played hide and seek with the sun. "Looks like we might not need the umbrella."

"Maybe not." Ethan spread out the blanket and put the basket and cooler on the edges. "Do you want one of the chairs?"

"No, the blanket is fine." She sank down onto it and crossed her legs, glad she'd nixed the sundress.

He plopped down beside her, then glanced

up. "Hope those clouds stay over there." He pointed at the grayish clouds gathering in the distance.

"Me, too."

She opened the basket and spread out the feast.

Ethan laughed. "Guess we should have asked a few more people to come along."

"I know. I overpacked." She blushed slightly at the enormity of the meal spread before them.

"Not a problem. I'll do my best." He reached for a sandwich.

They sat for an hour or so. For a welcome change, the time whisked past instead of crawling by. She relaxed and just enjoyed spending time with Ethan. Chatting. Laughing.

A rumble of thunder sounded in the distance as the clouds gathered and huddled above them.

"I guess we are going to get that storm after all." She glared at the clouds, not wanting them to ruin the wonderful time she was having. A really wonderful time after all that useless worrying and nerves this morning.

"We should probably pack up so we don't

get caught out in it." He rose and held out a hand for her.

She grabbed hold of his strong hand as he helped her to her feet. He kept her hand in his for a moment longer than necessary, and her heart fluttered as he stared at her.

"I wish the storm had stayed away. I'm not ready for the picnic to end," he said softly, his eyes glowing with an intensity that took her breath away.

A few large raindrops plopped on the blanket around them and practical thinking took over. "I'm not ready for it to end either, but I think we should hurry."

They gathered their things and stuffed them on the wagon as more raindrops plunked around them, making tiny indents in the sand.

"I don't think we're going to make it," Ethan said as he led the way across the sand, tugging the wagon behind them.

The storm did *not* wait for them, and the rain began in earnest as the thunder roared across the sky. Lightning flashed.

"Hurry, let's get to safety." He grabbed her hand, and they picked up the pace.

The rain let loose in full force as they raced

toward his house. Her clothes clung to her as they sprinted the distance, tugging the wagon across the wet sand and down the walkway.

They climbed the stairs, and he dumped the wet items from the wagon onto the porch. "Come on, let's get you inside."

She shivered slightly and shook out her wet hair, hanging in clumps around her shoulders. It probably looked like wet seaweed, and she probably looked like a bedraggled puppy. Not exactly how she thought this date would end.

Melody and Ethan stepped inside his home, dripping water all over the rug by his door. She shivered again.

"Let me get us some towels." Ethan disappeared, then came back with a stack of towels in his arms.

He handed her one—a big, fluffy, navy one —and she reached up to dry her sopping hair. The nice fluffy towel surprised her. For some reason, she half expected a bachelor to have old worn towels. He dropped another towel around her shoulders.

"You're soaked. How about I find you some dry clothes and we'll pop your clothes in the dryer?"

The chill spiraled through her. "Yes. Please."

He led her back to his bedroom and she ran her gaze around the room. A king-sized bed was centered between two large windows. A simple navy-striped spread covered the bed. An overstuffed chair and ottoman with a table beside them sat in the corner. A stack of magazines rested on the table. A wooden dresser with a polished top stood against another wall. A picture of Ethan—much younger—and another young man who looked very similar to him sat on top of the dresser. Maybe his brother? Nothing was really out of place, but the room looked lived-in and inviting.

He opened his closet and took out a terrycloth robe. "Here's an extra-large t-shirt you can put on, and this robe over it. Help yourself to whatever you need in the bathroom."

"Thank you."

"Just let me grab some dry clothes for me and I'll give you some privacy." He opened a drawer and took out a pair of sweatpants and a t-shirt, then disappeared out the door, pulling it firmly closed behind him.

She walked into the bathroom and looked in the mirror. Yikes. She did look like a bedraggled puppy. Slipping out of her wet clothes, she left them in a puddle on the tile floor. After briskly drying off, then attempting to dry her hair a bit more, she slipped on the t-shirt. It reached her knees and smelled faintly of wood and spice. She pressed the fabric to her face, inhaling the scent, and smiled. It smelled just like Ethan.

Feeling a bit like a voyeur, she opened his medicine cabinet and peeked inside, not sure what she was looking for. She closed it and opened the drawer near the sink and snagged a comb. Running the comb through her tangled hair, she finally managed to wrangle it into some semblance of non-bedraggled. Kind of.

She wrapped the robe around her, tying the belt securely around her waist. Bending down to scoop up the wet clothes, she took one last look in the mirror. No, this was not exactly the look she'd planned for this date.

She walked out of the room and found Ethan in the kitchen. A worn shirt stretched across his broad shoulders. The sweats sat on his hips. How had she never noticed he was in such good shape?

He padded over to her on bare feet. "I put on the kettle for some hot tea. It should be ready soon, and we'll get you warmed up."

"Sounds good."

"Here, hand me your clothes and I'll put them in the dryer if that's okay?" He eyed her.

"I can do it." Did she really want him putting her underthings in the dryer? It seemed so... intimate.

He reached for her bundle of clothes. "I don't mind. Go sit on the couch. There's a quilt on the back of it you can use if you're still chilled. I'll bring out tea in a minute."

She did as she was told, wandering out to the great room and settling on the sofa with her legs tucked beneath her. The storm raged outside, flashes of lightning illuminating the room and then plunging it back into low light.

She'd never been inside Ethan's house before. It suited him. Comfortable. Understated. Tidy.

He walked into the room and set the tea on the coffee table. "I'll get some lights on." He flicked on a lamp in the corner that spread its glow around the room but wasn't overpowering. It just made the room all that much cozier.

She reached for her tea and took a sip. The liquid rolled down her throat, bringing its welcome warmth. "Thanks for this." She set her cup down.

Ethan crossed over and sat down beside her. "You still look cold. Want the quilt?"

She nodded, and he settled the it over their laps and placed his arm around her shoulder. "Better?"

"Mm-hmm…" She could hardly speak. A layer of intimacy wrapped around them, just like the blanket.

"My grandma made this quilt. I know it's a bit worn, but it's been well-loved."

"I think it's lovely." She fingered the worn fabric and admired the even stitches.

"Grandma loved to quilt. And knit. And draw. I think she never met an art or craft she didn't enjoy."

"Did you inherit any of that talent?"

He laughed. "Nope. Not a bit."

"I don't do any of that either. Though Rose offered to teach me how to knit. I might take her up on it."

They sat in companionable silence for a bit, sipping their tea and watching the storm rage outside. When he got up to refill their cups, she was surprised by the sudden pang of longing for his presence that shot through her. She was thankful when he returned a moment later and settled beside her again.

He leaned back and stretched out his long legs. "Sorry about the abrupt end to the picnic. It sure was fun, though. You know, what there was of it." His lips curled in a small, familiar smile.

Her breath caught in her throat. She reached out for her cup and picked it up, hoping Ethan didn't notice the slight shake of her hands.

But he did and rescued the cup before she could spill anything, setting it back on the table.

"Melody?"

"Yes?" She looked into his clear blue eyes, seeing something in them smoldering in their depths.

"You know how I said I chickened out of kissing you the other night on our first date?"

She nodded slowly, still staring into his eyes. Mesmerized by them.

"I regret that very much."

"You do?" She swallowed.

"Yes, and I'd like very much to kiss you now… and not chicken out." His lips curved into that intimate smile again.

"I… uh…"

"Would that be okay with you?"

Time stood still while so many thoughts rushed through her mind. The past and present intertwined. Was she ready for this?

"It's okay if you want to say no. If it's too much."

She sucked in a deep breath and pulled her hand out from under the afghan, reaching up to touch his cheek. "No. I mean, yes. I mean, a kiss would be fine."

He lowered his lips to hers and kissed her gently. With a mind of its own, her hand wrapped around to the back of his neck. He pulled her closer and deepened the kiss. Her heart beat as wildly as waves crashing ashore in the storm as she lost herself in his kiss.

He finally pulled away, and she loosened her grip on his neck, dropping her hand to his shoulder. He stared right into her eyes. "You okay?"

Was she okay? She shouldn't be thinking about John, but she was. Ethan's kiss was… different… than John's. But it was so strange to kiss someone who wasn't John.

He reached out and touched her cheek and wiped away a tear she didn't know was there. "It's okay, you know. For it to feel strange to you. Different."

How did he know her exact thoughts? She nodded. "But it was… nice. Very nice." Her cheeks warmed. She wasn't good at this whole dating thing.

"If it was too much, we can slow down."

"That's probably a good idea." She nodded. Only she wanted him to kiss her again. Just didn't know how to ask him.

"Slow it is, then." He smiled, picked up her tea, and handed it to her. "Here, maybe this will help warm you."

Though right now she didn't need anything to warm her up. Heat surged through her, electric and sizzling. His kiss had awakened something she thought she'd never feel again. Didn't want to feel because she couldn't bear to lose everything again.

But she couldn't deny it. She did have feelings for Ethan. She did.

He got up and walked over to the window, looking outside at the storm that was finally beginning to fade, then turned back around to face her. "I've got all the time in the world, Mel. All the time. There's no hurry here."

And that's all she wanted. Time.

Or was it?

CHAPTER 5

J ack pulled up to his mother's house precisely at six. Thank goodness the storm had rolled away. It had put a damper on his whole plan for fresh air this afternoon, but there'd still been plenty to do.

He bounded up the stairs, and the door swung open before he had a chance to knock. "I'm ready, Jackson." His mother stood in the doorway, then turned and locked the door behind her.

No one could say his mother wasn't punctual, a trait he took pride in emulating. When they were growing up, she always told him and Shane the importance of being on

time. Over the years, he'd gotten almost as
pedantic about being on time as his mom.

They rode to the wharf, and he found a
parking space close to the entrance. As they
walked down the long wharf, his mother
occasionally stopped and peered into a window
of a shop. Mentioning the new tea and coffee
shop had a good selection. And the dress shop
had so many all-white outfits and she just wasn't
into that. She preferred to shop at Barbara's
Boutique downtown. Oh, and the candy store
had the best taffy now.

They reached the end of the wharf and
went into Jimmy's. It was one of his favorite
spots to eat in Moonbeam, and he was certain
his mother picked it because she knew that fact.
It wasn't fancy. Just simple, great food.

Walker Bodine, the owner's son, greeted
them as they entered. "Mrs. Rayburn, Jack.
Great to see you."

"Hello, Walker," his mother answered. "Are
your folks here tonight?"

"They're supposedly taking the night off, but
I won't be surprised if they pop in."

"If they do, tell your mother to stop by my
table. I finally found the recipe she asked me for.

It's for a cake I made for the women's group last week. I'd filed it away under breads, not desserts, in my recipe box. How silly of me."

"I'll tell her."

Walker led them to a four-top table near the railing. Not one of the high tops, though. Which was nice because he wasn't sure about his mother climbing up on those high barstools. Though she was still pretty spry.

He held out the chair for her and she sat down, placing her purse on the chair beside her. He took a seat across from her.

"Looks like we might still manage a nice sunset. That was quite the storm that blew through, wasn't it?" Walker handed them menus.

"It was." He nodded.

He glanced across the distance and spied Daisy as she stepped out onto the outdoor deck. She stood in the entryway, alone. Without thinking, he waved and caught her attention. She smiled and came over to their table.

"Well, hello again."

"Mom, do you know Daisy?"

"Ah, the owner of our new flower shop. No, I've heard of her, but we haven't met."

"Mom, this is Daisy. Daisy, this is my mother, Mona."

"Nice to meet you, Mona." Daisy greeted his mother with a wide, warm smile.

"And it's nice to meet you. I suppose you were the one who made the lovely corsage that Jackson gave me today."

"I did. I hope you liked it. And happy birthday, by the way."

"Thank you. It was very pretty. I have it in the fridge now, hoping to make it last a bit longer. I'll take it out and put it on my table in the morning while I drink my coffee. It will look so nice and cheerful there."

"Are you here alone?" Jack looked up at Daisy.

"Yes. It's just me."

"Would you like to join us?" he asked, hoping she'd say yes, but not certain why he wanted her to so badly.

"I don't want to interrupt your birthday celebration."

"It's not an interruption. We'd love to have you join us." His mom motioned to the empty chair beside him. "Please, sit down."

He jumped up and pulled out the chair, and

Daisy took a seat. Walker came by and dropped off another place setting and menu and laughed. "Busy night tonight. Looks like I'm greeter, waiter, and I've been helping in the kitchen, too."

Jack was a bit envious that Walker seemed so comfortable in all those roles. That he fit in. As Walker strode away from the table, he paused to greet another group of customers. A woman hugged him, her face beaming. A man pumped Walker's hand and clapped him on the back like they were long-lost friends. Yes, it was clear Walker belonged here. But then, he'd been born and raised here.

There was no reason to think Jack should fit in like Walker did. He'd only been here for a little while. He'd make friends eventually. And hopefully they wouldn't all be his mother's age… which described most people he'd met so far.

Except for Daisy. He smiled at her, and she smiled back, putting him at ease. Suddenly, he was way more excited about this dinner.

Daisy had been expecting to eat alone, as usual. She even had a book tucked in her purse to keep her company while she ate. Now she was going to eat with Jack and Mona instead. A welcome departure from dining alone so often. She just wasn't that social or very adept at making friends. Besides, she'd been so busy with the flower shop.

But this was nice. Company during a meal.

They all ordered and sat sipping their drinks. The sun put on a glorious display for them as the storm clouds scattered away into the distance.

"I never tire of the sunsets over the bay," Mona said.

"They're quite remarkable." Daisy glanced out over the water again. She didn't know why the sunsets looked so different here than in Colorado. But they did. At least to her. She should miss the mountains with the brilliant sunsets painting their peaks… but instead, she couldn't bear to even think about the mountains. Couldn't watch a movie with mountains. Hadn't watched a Colorado sports team since she rolled out of the state, even though before she'd watched more games than she could count.

Before... *it* happened. But she'd vowed not to think about that anymore.

So she wouldn't. She shoved away the memories, turned toward Jack, and put on a big smile. "So, are you getting all packed up for your move?"

The smile he gave her was warm and friendly. "There's not much to pack. What little furniture I had before I moved here is in storage. It's nice that Mr. Cooper is renting his place furnished. If I find a more permanent place later, I'll get my things shipped here. But for now, I don't have to deal with that."

Mrs. Rayburn shook her head. "I love having my things around me. So many memories. I still have the same wooden table where you and your brother would sit and do homework."

"I'm well aware, Mom. I think we've had to fix the legs on it a half dozen times. Shane and I keep telling you to just get a new one."

"I wouldn't dream of it. I love that table."

"Just kidding, Mom. I know you won't part with it. And I kind of like still seeing it in the kitchen when I come over. What can I say? Guess I have a bit of a nostalgic soul."

Daisy thought about her own home now. All new furniture. Well, most of it was from thrift stores, but still new to her. She'd sold or given away all her furniture in Colorado when she headed out on her travels, exploring places and deciding where to settle down. She hadn't wanted anything that would remind her of that old life.

You're thinking about it again.

Mona set her drink on the table, oblivious to Daisy's bouncing thoughts." I still have a few boxes of your things in the guest closet, Jackson. You should come and look through them. See what you want."

"I'll do that, Mom."

Their meal was delivered, and as they ate, Mona regaled them with stories of the people of Moonbeam. Like the infamous Jenkins twins, who seemed to know everyone's business. Daisy had met them. They'd popped into her shop and welcomed her when she first came to town, asking her a million questions, which she answered in a vague way, not wanting everyone to know everything about her. And specifically not answering their one big question. Why had she moved to Moonbeam?

"And you know Walker, right?" Mona asked. "His father, Jimmy, owns the restaurant, but Walker and his sister Tara are slowly taking over."

"You sound like you know everyone," Daisy said.

"I've been here a lot of years. My husband and I retired down here. But he passed away."

"I'm sorry."

"Oh, it's been some time now. And my son, Shane, came to live in Moonbeam. Then when he moved away this year for a new job, Jackson came to live here. But as I told both the boys, I don't need someone living here in the same town. They should live their own lives. I'm perfectly capable of taking care of myself."

Daisy didn't doubt it for a moment. Mona seemed sharp and in good shape and genuinely happy to live here in Moonbeam.

"Mom, I like living down here. The weather is great. And besides, this way I get lots of good home-cooked meals." Jack winked.

Mona shook her head. "My boys both love me for my cooking."

"Yep, the only reason." Jack nodded, smothering a smile.

Daisy was the tiniest bit jealous of the easy relationship the two had. She wasn't close to any family. Wasn't close to anyone, really. Not anymore.

"Let me pay the bill, and we should go. It's getting late," Mona said as she motioned to Walker.

"Mom, it's eight o'clock." Jack shook his head.

"I know. Like I said, it's getting late."

Walker came over. "Can I get you anything else?"

"Just the check, please. I'm buying," Mona said with a firm tone.

Jack started to interrupt, but Mona held up her hand. "No, I'm buying for all of us. Don't argue. Being an old lady has its privileges."

"You don't have to buy my dinner," Daisy protested.

"I know I don't have to. I want to."

Mona paid, and they all rose. "Now, did you walk or drive here, Daisy?"

"I walked. I walk everywhere. I love that about Moonbeam."

"Well, like I said, it's getting late. Jack will drop me off, then drive you home."

"He doesn't have to do that."

Jack leaned close, grinning. "Best not to argue with Mom. You'll never win."

They all strolled down the wharf and out to Jack's car. When they dropped off Mona, he walked her to her door and made sure she got inside okay. Then they headed to her cottage.

"I want to thank you for inviting me to join you for dinner. It was really nice. And it was nice having your mom talk about the town and who everyone is. I'm still trying to find my footing here."

"I know the feeling. Like an outsider. Not that the people aren't friendly." Jack pulled into her drive and came around to open her door. She slid out, and they climbed up on her porch.

"Thank you again."

"You're welcome. Glad you joined us." He stood there waiting.

"Oh." She unlocked her door and turned back. "There, see? All safe and sound."

He grinned. "Good. Well, good night, then."

"Good night, Jack. See you around."

She watched him drive away and went into her cottage, flipping on the lamp. She dropped her purse on the table, then wandered into the kitchen and put a kettle on for some tea. Once she had a steaming mug in hand, she took it over to the window to look outside. The moon sparkled on the water with no sign of the torrential rain and lightning storm of this afternoon. But then, she'd learned that was how Florida was. A storm rolled in and just as quickly would roll away.

It had been so nice to have dinner with someone tonight instead of eating alone. The pleasant talk. The laughs. And Jack seemed like a genuinely nice guy. He certainly treated his mother well, and they both seemed to enjoy each other's company.

Yes, it had been an interesting evening. And now she was confident that she wouldn't mind having Jack as a neighbor. They might even become friends, and then she wouldn't have to eat alone quite so often. Maybe she should cook him a welcoming meal. Except she wasn't that great of a cook. Just the basics. But she could pick up dinner and take it to him for his first night in the new place. That might be a good idea.

She wandered back into the kitchen and set the cup in the sink, turning out the light as she left the room. She went down the hall in her silent house and plopped down on her bed.

Life was really different now. But it had been her choice to leave Colorado. Not run away, she assured herself, just *move*. And she didn't regret it. She was certain she'd made the right decision. Mostly.

CHAPTER 6

Melody sat in her favorite chair, sipping chamomile tea. Ethan had dropped her off at her cottage after her clothes finally dried. He'd walked her to the door... and there was no good-night kiss.

No kiss.

But that's what she wanted. What she told him she wanted. To slow things down. Even so, a little good-night kiss never hurt anything, did it?

She closed her eyes, shaking her head at her jumbled thoughts. Brief flashes from the day skipped through her mind. Getting caught in the rain. Sitting and talking quietly at his house.

The kiss. Of course, the kiss. The way his lips felt against hers.

She set the cup down with a clatter, jumped up, and paced the room. Back and forth, restless. The memories of the day playing like a movie through her mind.

The light from one lamp tossed low rays around the room. She flipped on another lamp, brightening the space, chasing away any hint of darkness. So many thoughts crowded her brain, twisting between memories of John and thoughts of today with Ethan. Caught between two lives, two realities.

She spun around and crossed over to the shelf unit, running her hands along the spines of the books. Most of them were John's. Some old hardbacks with worn leather covers. Some nonfiction on a variety of subjects. He was always learning about something new. Some were the paperback spy thrillers and mysteries that he loved so much. None of them were her type of reading, but she'd never gotten rid of them.

She touched another spine, worn from the many times John had read the book. Her heart squeezed in her chest.

It was silly to keep the books, selfish even, because someone would love to read them. Filled with resolution, she went and found a box and started to slowly pack up the books, determined to give them a new life with someone who would love them. She ended up keeping only five, one a book of poetry he would sometimes read to her. As she opened the book, a paper slipped out and fell to the floor. She smiled, knowing it was another of his notes.

She leaned down and picked it up. Slowly, she read the words. But this was not like his usual love notes.

~

My dearest Melody,

~

I know you'll find this note just when you're meant to. This wasn't the way I planned our life together. Our time together was cut way too short. But just know that I loved you with my very soul. I'm so, so sorry to leave you. It looks like life had other plans for us.

But you must go on and live your life. I want the

world for you. Filled with all the happiness and joy. Do that for me, my love.

~

All my love forever,
   John

~

She clutched the note to her heart as tears began to flow. But this time, the tears were less sadness and loss, and more healing. As the tears trailed off, she walked over to the chair and sat down. Opening the book to one of her favorite poems, she ran her fingers over the words.

She took the note and tucked it back into the book. She would do what John asked. Live her life.

He'd given her his blessing to find happiness, and that was just what she was going to do. Or at least she was going to give it a good try.

CHAPTER 7

Rose sat out watching the sunrise. The soft light from the sunrise to the east reflected in the clouds and water here on the west coast. As usual, it didn't disappoint. Faint streaks of pink lightly colored the clouds. The waves rolled slowly to shore as the birds chased each other, silhouetted against the brightening sky.

She'd miss this when she went back home. Sighing, she picked up a shell from beside her on the beach. Delicate veins of lilac laced through it. One tiny chip graced its edge. Not perfect, but pretty and still hanging in there. It looked like it had lived a good life. She smiled at the thought.

A lone runner a bit down the beach eased his pace and slowed to a jog, heading her way.

She lifted her hand in a friendly wave. He jogged up to her. "Morning. Looks like we're the only two out enjoying the sunrise this morning."

"Looks like it. I'm out most mornings, though."

He turned and looked out over the water. "Pretty nice reflection of the sunrise, isn't it? I almost decided to run over to the bay to see if I could catch a better view, but this is nice."

"It is. And have you seen the sunsets here? Just glorious."

"Saw a great one last night while eating at Jimmy's."

"I think I saw you at Violet's cottages, didn't I?"

"You did. Been staying there a few days."

"I'm there, too." The woman held out her hand. "Rose. I'm in the last cottage. The peach one."

He took her hand in his. "Jack. Nice to meet you. I'm in the green cottage. I think Violet called it *mint* green."

"She does like her colorful cottages." Rose smiled. "Are you staying long?"

"I'm actually moving out on Wednesday. Found a place to rent. It's just down the beach." He tilted his head back the way he had come.

"I'm a bit of a permanent fixture around here. I came to stay at the cottages at the beginning of September, and I haven't left. I do need to make my way back home soon, though."

"It's a nice town. I can see why you've stayed."

"Did you move here for work?"

"Ah, not really. My mother lives here. Mona Rayburn. I can work from anywhere, so I decided to move here to be closer. I don't really like leaving her here alone. Even though she insists she doesn't need me here, I think she enjoys it."

"I'm sure she does. You're lucky to have family nearby."

"I am. Now if I could just meet more people my age." He grinned. "I've spent a lot of time with Mom and her friends."

"It takes a while to meet people and begin to fit in."

"I guess so. I'm quite the outsider here, I fear. Even with Mom living here."

"Bet you won't feel like that for long. Violet practically adopted me as part of her family since I've been here. And I've met so many people." And it was nice to feel like she had family again. *Almost* family.

"I guess I've been busy working and trying to find a place to live and I just haven't taken time to get to know people."

"You should if you're going to live here. It's always nice to have friends."

"I have met one. Well, I guess you'd call her a friend. Daisy. She owns the flower shop."

"Oh, I know Daisy. A lovely woman. And she's a wonder with flowers."

"She is. Made a very pretty corsage for my mom. For her birthday."

"That was a sweet gift for your mother."

"Actually, it was my brother's idea. I guess he used to give her one every year when he lived here. He's moved away." He shrugged. "And it looks like I'm going to be Daisy's neighbor."

"That's good. So you'll have someone to borrow a cup of sugar from." Rose smiled.

He laughed. "Yes, I guess I will."

"And you can consider me a friend, too. I'm

here every morning. If you're out for a run, just stop on by."

"Thanks, Rose. I'll do that." He glanced at his watch. "I better go grab a shower. I've got a meeting for work in about half an hour. It was nice meeting you."

"You, too."

Jack jogged away toward the cottages. What a nice young man. Moving here to be closer to his mother. And getting her flowers. She hoped he made friends here soon. A young man like that needed friends and people to hang out with. At least he had his mother here with him.

It must be so nice to live around family. She hadn't had that since she'd married Emmett. Well, Emmett was family, just not the family she was born into. But he was gone now, too.

But if she was being totally honest with herself, she did have family. Still. Well, she probably did. A pang grabbed hold and caught in her chest, flooding her with memories. Her sister, Pauline, wading at the beach with her. Flying a kite on a warm spring day. Sharing their clothes. Talking about boys. They'd been so very close growing up.

Until they weren't.

She thought again about trying to find Pauline, but her last attempt had ended in failure. Then again, she hadn't tried very hard.

But as the years went on, it seemed a bit frivolous to throw away what remaining family she had. Some things were hard to forgive, maybe impossible. But was there a possibility of some kind of truce, even if everything wasn't exactly forgotten?

She didn't know.

Melody hurried over to Blue Heron Cottages. If she got there early enough, she could have coffee with Violet and Rose.

As she approached the office, Rose waved to her. "Come sit. Violet just went in to answer the phone. She'll be back out soon."

Melody sat beside Rose. Violet poked her head out. "I'm getting more coffee. Mel, you want some?"

"Yes, thank you."

Violet came out a minute later, handed her a cup, and leaned against the railing. "So, it's a good thing you came over this morning. Rose and I were just wondering about your date with Ethan. Was it fabulous?"

"It was…" She didn't really know how to describe it. Wonderful. Scary. Fabulous. Unsettling. "It was great. I had a really good time."

"Did the storm cut it short?" Rose asked.

"We actually got caught out in it. Got soaked. We went to Ethan's house and got dry."

"And? Is that all we're going to get?" Violet teased.

Melody laughed. "The picnic was nice. We sat and chatted and he's just so easy to be with. Had a great time. But then we headed off the beach when the storm came. But like I said, got caught out in the rain. He gave me dry clothes to change into. He made hot tea. We talked while my clothes were in the dryer."

"That's all? Talked?" Violet raised an eyebrow.

She blushed and looked down at her coffee cup.

"That's what I thought. Tell us more." Violet sank onto the chair beside her.

"He… he kissed me."

"I knew it." Violet snapped her fingers.

"It was nice..." She looked away for a moment, almost feeling his lips still on hers. "But... it was different. Kind of strange to kiss someone who wasn't John."

"I'm sure it was," Rose said softly.

"Anyway..." She straightened up in her chair. "He offered for us to take things slowly. I said that's what I wanted. And he was fine with that. Said he'd give me all the time in the world."

"That's good, right?" Violet tilted her head.

"It is... and yet... I thought he'd still kiss me good night. Or something. Oh, I don't know. I'm obviously just a confused, crazy woman."

"No, you're not. You have every right to not know exactly how this will go. How you feel. Being a widow... that's very hard." Rose's eyes were filled with sympathy and understanding. "And to then date again? Your whole world is changing."

"It is hard. But there's more..."

"What?" Violet jumped up and leaned against the railing again, staring at her.

"I got home, and I was restless. I decided..." She took a deep breath, then continued with the same sense of resolve that had filled her last night. "I decided to pack up all John's books to give away. I mean, I'm not reading them. I only kept a few books. One was a book of poetry he read to me often. And… a note fell out of it."

"What did it say?" Rose leaned over and placed her hand over hers.

"He must have written it right before… before he died. He knew I'd go read my favorite poem again sometime." She couldn't help but smile at the thought. "The note said how much he loved me. But he wanted me to live my life. To find happiness again."

"He sounds like a wonderful man. Selfless. Giving." Rose patted her hand.

"He was wonderful." It surprised Melody that no tears fell now, like they usually did when she thought so deeply about John. It was more of a warm feeling, a good feeling. Filled with the wonderful memories of the good times they'd shared.

"So… are you going to? Start living your life? Find happiness? Maybe with Ethan?" Violet cocked her head to the side, staring closely at her.

"I… I am going to start living life. Not just going through the motions like I feel like I've done the last few years. I've been better since I started working at Parker's General Store and the cafe. But still, not really enjoying the moments. You know?"

"I know." Rose nodded. "I know only too well. I'm trying very hard to enjoy the simple moments in life. To... live. To move on. Not that I'll ever forget my Emmett. But there is still life to live. Days to enjoy."

Melody nodded. "There are. And I plan on enjoying them more, not just pass through each day. I feel... I feel like I can finally breathe again."

Violet came over and hugged her. "You're a smart woman, Melody. Strong. I predict great things are coming your way."

She wrapped her arms around Violet. "I hope so." She pulled in a deep breath of the fresh air. The day seemed brighter today. Fuller. She hoped Ethan would stop by the cafe today for dinner. She couldn't wait to see him again.

CHAPTER 8

"Ellen, are you sure you're going to be okay here alone?" Daisy asked as she glanced around the shop late Wednesday afternoon, making sure everything was in place.

"I'll be fine. Really. I have those bouquets to make up, but you've already made the first one, so I'll just duplicate what you did."

For the hundredth time, Daisy thanked her lucky stars for finding Ellen to help out at her shop. She'd realized she couldn't do everything anymore. Run the shop, do the arrangements, do the deliveries. And Ellen was really talented with flowers and a hard worker. She was new to town, too, so they bonded over being the newbies in Moonbeam. She'd lived in Tampa before moving here and had worked with a florist there for years.

Things couldn't be going better. The town had embraced her store, eager to have a floral shop in town. She was confident that she could really make a go of things here. She'd picked the right town to settle down in.

"Okay. Thanks. You can close up at six, okay?"

"I've got it. Really. Go." Ellen grinned, shaking her head and motioning her to leave.

She grabbed her purse and headed out. She wanted to pick up the dinner she'd ordered from Sea Glass Cafe and run it over to Jack's new place. As a thank-you for asking her to join him and Mona the other night. That was all. Sandwiches, a few sides, and slices of pie for dessert. She had to eat, too, right?

She pushed into the cafe, and Melody waved to her. "I've got your order. Just a sec."

Melody disappeared into the kitchen and came back with a sack of food. She rang her up. "Dinner for two, huh?" Melody smiled. "That's nice."

"I... uh... I have a new neighbor. He's moving in today. Going to give him dinner, and then I figured I'd order for me, too."

"Is that Mona's son? Jackson, is it? She was in here earlier saying he was renting Mr. Cooper's place. Moving in today."

"Yes, it's for Jack."

"Okay, hang on a second." Melody disappeared into the kitchen and returned with another sack. "I packed him up some cinnamon rolls for his breakfast tomorrow. Tell him it's a little housewarming gift from Sea Glass Cafe."

"Thank you. I will." She took the sacks and headed out to her car. She drove home and popped into the cottage, setting the food on the counter. After changing clothes and fixing her hair just a bit—okay, and putting on a bit of makeup—she picked up the food and headed to Mr. Cooper's. Or, really, it was Jack's, now.

She walked around to the front door and knocked. Then knocked again a little louder when no one answered. Jack's car was parked in front of the house, but that didn't mean much. So many people walked all over the town. Maybe she was too late, and he'd walked to go have dinner. Or see his mother. Disappointment that she had no right to feel flooded through her. She was just doing a friendly favor.

She started to turn to leave, and the door flew open.

"Oh, I thought maybe someone knocked. Wasn't sure. I was back in the bedroom putting clothes away." He smiled at her. "What do we have here?"

"I picked up some dinner for you. I mean, if you don't have plans. And Melody from Sea Glass Cafe put in some cinnamon rolls for your breakfast as a housewarming gift. Your mother told her you were moving in today."

"Mom is quite the announcer of my business." He laughed, reached out, and took the food from her. "Come in. I'm famished."

She followed him into the house, not sure why she thought it would look any different from the times she'd been in Mr. Cooper's house before.

"This was really nice of you. I did pick up a few things, staple items mostly, from the market. Nothing to make for dinner. I was planning to go out to eat yet again."

"Now you don't have to." She followed him

into the kitchen. "Oh, and my dinner is in there, too, if that's okay. And I thought maybe you'd like some help unpacking?"

"You don't have to do that. But I'd love company for dinner." He opened the sack and took out the sandwiches, sides, and pie. "Looks great."

"Plates?" she asked.

He laughed. "No clue. Go ahead and open cabinets. I've only loaded the fridge and the pantry."

She opened the cabinets until she found two plates, then found the silverware drawer. "Here we go."

"Want to eat outside? It's nice out."

"Sure. Sounds good."

"And I picked up some red wine. A merlot. Would you like a glass?"

"I'd love that." She placed their food on the plates and took them outside. He followed shortly with the wine.

As they settled at the table, he lifted his glass. "To new neighbors."

"New neighbors." She lightly touched her glass to his.

Jack attacked his sandwich with gusto. "This is so good."

"Wait until you try the peach pie. So delicious. And you won't be disappointed with your cinnamon rolls tomorrow, either."

"I'll have to remember the cafe. I've been to a few places. Love Jimmy's on the Wharf. And I went to The Cabot Hotel for a fancy dinner with Mom once. And Brewster's. They have great coffee."

"I've heard that, but haven't gone there yet." So many places for her to try, and places she wanted to see. Mostly she'd just buried herself in her work getting the shop open.

"We'll have to grab coffee there some morning before work." He said the words casually, like it was no big deal.

Was it? Was it like a coffee date? Or just friends meeting for coffee? "We'll have to." That was all she could think of to reply.

"So, Mr. Cooper gave me a break on rent when he mentioned that he'd wanted to paint the place before he rented it. I said I'd paint it for him. And I've already fixed a door that wouldn't close on the closet." He laughed. "I'm kind of a fixer guy, so if you need anything, I'm your man."

"I'll keep that in mind."

"Got the utilities and internet switched over to my name. I think I'm about set. Though Mom said she had a big box of things she'd packed up for me to make it feel more like home. I'll run by and get it tomorrow."

"I bet she loves having you living here."

"Not that she'd admit it over all her protests that I didn't have to move here. But really, I can work from anywhere. Moonbeam seemed like as good a place as any to put down roots for a while." He picked up his glass and leaned back in his chair, his plate empty. "So what brought you to Moonbeam?"

"I... ah..." That was always a question she had no idea how to answer. "I was traveling around and visited here. Really liked it. So I moved here." That was kind of the truth in a half-truth kind of way.

"And the shop is doing okay? Mom loved her corsage."

"It's busy. I hired someone to help out. I was trying to balance everything and I just couldn't. Not with deliveries, and making the arrangements, ordering flowers, paying bills, and all of that. Ellen. She's really great."

"Glad you could find help."

Silence drifted between them as she scrambled to think of what to say. "So, what do you do? For work I mean?"

"I'm a techie sort of guy. Various techie things. Programming. Web design. Custom online storefronts for online businesses."

"I only know the basics. I do have a website for my business. It's functional and I think it's pretty." She laughed. "Nothing fancy, though. I do get a few online orders to be delivered, but most people come into the shop."

"Hey, I found you by searching online. I also —" His phone rang, and he pulled it from his pocket and glanced at it. "Sorry, it's Mom. Do you mind?"

"No, that's fine."

He answered the call. "Hey, Mom. Yes, I'm all moved in. No, I'm fine."

Silence while he listened to his mother. "No, I swear. I'm eating dinner right now. I won't starve." He shook his head. "I'll come over tomorrow and pick up that box."

Another long pause while he listened.

"Okay, yes. I'd love to have dinner at your place tomorrow. I'll be over after work. Okay. See you then." He placed the phone on the table. "Sorry about that. But if I don't answer when she thinks I should, she starts to worry. I keep trying to get her to text me, but she says she doesn't like it. If I text her, she calls me back." He shrugged. "I'm not sure she's much into cell phones. Still uses her landline when she's at home."

"I don't mind. She probably just worries about you."

"She thinks I'm going to starve to death living on my own." His eyes twinkled with his smile. "Wonder what she thought I was doing all those years when I didn't live so close to her?"

"But now she knows more about your day-to-day life."

"She does." A wry smile tipped the corners of his mouth. "I'm not sure how I feel about that. I'm fairly certain she doesn't realize I'm a grown man."

"I guess you'll both have to do some adjusting. Figure it out."

"We will." He reached for the bottle of wine

and poured himself another glass. "You?" He held up the bottle.

"Maybe a half glass."

He poured some of the deep red liquid into the glass she held out. She took a sip before setting the glass on the table. "Ready for the pie?"

"You bet."

She dished them both up a piece of pie and took a bite, savoring the rich, cinnamony goodness tangled with the sweet tanginess of peaches. "I swear, this is the best peach pie ever."

"It really is." He took another bite. "But don't tell my mom I said that. She'll get her feelings hurt."

She crossed her heart. "I swear it will be our secret." She grinned at him, enjoying the easy conversation.

They finished their pie and their wine, and she helped him bring everything back inside. "Let me help with the dishes."

"That's okay. I'll get them. And it will give me time to find my way around the kitchen."

She nodded and just stood there, not really

wanting to leave but having no reason to stay. "Well, I guess I should go."

"I'll walk you home."

"It's only a few steps across the sand," she protested, then mentally chastised herself. If nothing else, it would be a few more minutes with him.

"Still, I'd like to walk you."

"Okay, sure." They headed outside, down his steps, and across the sand to her cottage. She stood on the bottom step of her deck. "Here I am. See, only a couple of steps away."

"I really do appreciate you bringing the dinner. And the company." He paused, his forehead wrinkled. "I don't suppose... suppose you'd like..."

He shifted from foot to foot in the sand.

"Could we do this again? I'm tired of eating out and eating alone. I could barbecue for us. Steaks?"

"That would be nice."

"Saturday night?"

"I'll see if Ellen can close up for me. Can I let you know?"

"Sure. Want to put my number in your phone and you can text me?"

He gave her his number, and she entered it into her phone, feeling comforted to have a neighbor's number now that Mr. Cooper was gone. She'd had his. Anyway, that was all it was.

She opened the door and gave him a little wave as she slipped inside. He turned and jogged the distance to his cottage.

And then she was alone with the silence yet again. She should be used to it by now. It's what she'd wanted, right? To live alone somewhere besides Colorado. She squeezed her eyes tight, refusing to let the tears flow. Not anymore. She was over the tears.

She slowly walked back to her bedroom and crawled onto the bed, pulling a quilt up over herself as she leaned against the pillows and stared into the darkness. She'd thought that getting a twin bed would help. That it wouldn't feel so huge and empty. But… that wasn't quite the truth. Even this tiny bed felt barren and desolate. She picked up a pillow and punched it, taking out her frustration at the unfairness of life before plopping it behind her back.

She wavered on the whole going over to dinner at Jack's. Did she really want to get involved with someone? Hadn't she learned her lesson? Her terrible, terrible lesson? But having some meals together didn't mean a relationship, now did it? It was just a dinner with a friend.

She resolutely leaned over, switched on the light, and picked up her e-reader beside her bed. Having a pity party didn't solve anything. Getting lost in a book just might.

CHAPTER 9

E than hadn't been in the cafe for three days, not that Melody was counting. If he didn't come in today, it would make four days. *Four days*.

Nor had he called. She'd heard nothing from him since Sunday. Of course, her phone worked, too. She could call or text him. But she wanted him to call her. To come into the cafe to see her. When he'd suggested they take it slow, she didn't think he meant *this* slowly.

She busied herself taking orders, helping cook, delivering orders, and chatting with customers. Anything to keep her mind off Ethan. But it was just going through the motions, the very thing she said she wasn't going to be doing anymore.

She was supposed to be living every moment. Enjoying life. Being happy. And yet, she was a bit sad, woeful, even dejected—and a million other words—with not seeing Ethan. And that annoyed her a bit. Hadn't she been perfectly content with her life before he asked her out?

Or had she?

Dating was confusing. A twisted path that tossed her in one direction, then the other. And she hated that. She needed some control. Knowing what comes next.

Or at the very least, she'd like him to come in and eat a meal like he used to.

Maybe he'd changed his mind about dating her? The thought struck a quiver of fear through her. She'd gotten so used to seeing him almost daily. Talking to him. Having him as a friend.

Had dating ruined all that? Just like she'd been afraid of?

She heard the door to the cafe open and whirled around, half-expecting to be disappointed yet again. But there he was, silhouetted in the doorway with the sun spilling inside around him. An automatic smile swept her lips into a wide grin.

He was here.

She hurried over to him, then paused, uncertain. "Uh… hi."

"Hi," he said softly, snatching off the ball cap he wore and grasping it in his hands.

"A table?" Had he come to eat? Or to see her? Or…

"Yes, thanks." Were his words curt? Brusque? Had he just come because he was hungry?

He followed her to a table in the corner and sat down, settling into his chair and placing his cap on the table. Then he moved the hat slightly, avoiding looking at her. Suddenly, he jumped back up. "Melody?"

"Yes?" She stared at the confused expression on his face.

"That was the hardest three days in history. I was trying to give you your space. But… I missed you." The earnestness was clear in his eyes, in the tone of his voice.

She reached out and touched his arm, connecting with him, as a jolt of emotion surged through her. "I... I missed you, too. I thought that..." She blushed slightly. "I thought that maybe you didn't want to date me anymore."

"Of course I want to date you." His sky-blue eyes pierced the distance between them. "Of course, I do. I was just slowing things down. Like you said you wanted."

"Too slow." She shook her head and gave him a wry smile. "Not seeing you for three days was just very... strange."

He let out a long sigh. "I'm not very good at this dating thing. I know that. I was trying to do what you wanted. To go slow."

"Slow didn't mean I don't want to see you. I miss you popping in here for meals. Talking with you."

"I'm so relieved to hear that. I've missed you. And let's just say my meals haven't been anything like what I get here at the cafe." A smile eased across his face.

She laughed. "How about I bring you your lunch?"

"That would be great." He sank onto his chair, relief sweeping over his features. "Just great. I'm starving."

She laughed. "I'll bring you today's special. You'll love it."

He caught her hand as she started to walk away. "Melody?"

"Yes?" His gaze caught and held hers.

"It would be fine with me if we don't ever do this whole three-days-apart thing again."

She stared at him for a moment, her heart fluttering before she slowly bobbed her head. "I think that would be fine with me, too."

Daisy greeted Ellen as she came in about noon to the flower shop. "Morning. Or I guess it's afternoon now."

Ellen walked over and pulled on a bright yellow apron with *Beach Blooms* embroidered on it. "Very busy this morning?"

"I did get an order for a wedding. It's in about six months." Daisy cut off the stem of a pink rose before placing it in the arrangement she was working on.

"A wedding is always good." Ellen walked over to the counter. "Oh, and after you left, the manager of Sunrise Village stopped in. She's thinking of doing their table centerpieces through you instead of having them delivered from Belle Island. I showed her some ideas, and she said she'd come by and talk directly to you."

"That would be a great bit of regular business. Hope it works out." And that was why she was always leery of leaving the shop, even though Ellen was very capable. People wanted to talk directly to her about things like this. But she just couldn't do it all herself. Maybe after they'd both worked here longer, people would trust both of them.

Ellen picked up the watering can and filled it. "So, how was your date with your neighbor last night?"

"It wasn't a date. I was just bringing him dinner."

"Okay, how was dinner last night?"

"It was fun. Enjoyed his company."

"So, are you seeing him again?"

"I'm sure I will. I mean, he's my neighbor."

"I meant as a date…" Ellen grinned. "Or a *dinner*."

"Just so happens he invited me over for a barbecue on Saturday. I said I had to check and see if you could close up."

"Works for me. You know I always love more hours. And it sure sounds like you're having a lot of *dinners* with him." Ellen smothered a smile.

Daisy ignored the dinner remark. "I said I'd text him and let him know." She grabbed her phone and sent off a text. She got a quick reply saying he'd see her then. She was kind of looking forward to it. But only because it was a break from eating alone. That was it.

Ellen didn't bother trying to hide her grin this time. "You're smiling now."

"I always smile. I'm a happy person," she retorted. But the smile continued to tug at the corners of her mouth, and she had to admit she was pleased to have the date with Jack. Well, the dinner with him.

CHAPTER 10

Saturday turned into a rainy day. Slightly colder than normal and very windy. Daisy wasn't sure if Jack would want to cancel the barbecue since the weather was so lousy, but he texted her late afternoon to make sure she was still coming. Said he'd made a big pot of chili instead of the steaks he'd promised and hoped that was okay. She assured him that was fine. It actually sounded pretty perfect for a day like today.

When she got home from work, she changed into slacks and a lightweight sweater. Different than the heavy cable-knit sweaters she'd left behind in Colorado.

Would she ever stop comparing things to Colorado?

Annoyed, she pushed the thought aside, dug around in her closet for the shoes she wanted, and slipped them on. She kind of missed boots, though. Hiking boots. Cute, simple boots with jeans. She'd even had two pairs of cowboy boots.

Colorado again. She rolled her eyes at herself. Slipping on her decidedly-not-boots red flats, she grabbed her cell phone off the dresser. She'd be right on time if she left now.

After grabbing an umbrella, she went out the front door and hurried along the sidewalk to Jack's house. She popped up onto his porch and shook out her umbrella, then leaned it against the wall for the walk back home. Before she could knock, the door flew open.

"There you are. Come in out of the rain." Jack grabbed her hand and tugged her inside. "Full day of rain and really chilly for this time of year, according to Mom."

"That's what Ellen said today at the shop. Unusual for this time of year." She followed him into the house, stopped, and stared in surprise. There was a fire going in the fireplace.

He saw her staring and laughed. "I know that not many houses down here have a fireplace. But I love a fire. Didn't start a very big one. Thought it might chase away the gloom."

She closed her eyes for a moment, fighting back emotions. Ignoring the cozy feel the dancing flames gave the room. She thought she'd be safe from fireplaces down here. From their enchantment. Their intimacy.

"You okay?" He narrowed his eyes in concern.

"What? Yes. Just a bit surprised by the fireplace is all." And comparing it to her life in Colorado, of course. Because that seemed like all she could do these days.

"Come into the kitchen while I finish making our dinner, then we can sit and have a glass of wine if you'd like. Or a beer."

"A beer sounds good." She followed him to the kitchen with one last glance at the dancing flames.

"I just need to finish the salad, and I picked up a loaf of homemade bread from the cafe." He grinned. "And I might have gotten some more cinnamon rolls. Those were so good."

"I got some this week, too," she admitted.

And they'd been wickedly delicious with their deep cinnamon flavor and sweet brown sugar mixed with the yeasty goodness of the dough.

He pulled two bottles of beer from the fridge and popped their tops off. "Glass?"

"Bottle is fine."

He handed her a bottle and took a swig from his own before turning toward the counter to continue the meal prep.

"The chili smells delicious."

He turned to her. "It's Mom's recipe, and I have to admit, I have it down to a science. It's really good."

He finished making the salad, set the bowl in the fridge, then led the way back into the family room. And the fireplace.

They sat on the couch across from the fire. It flickered, trying to lure her into enjoying the coziness of the room. A flash of lightning lit up the sky outside the window, competing with the flames inside.

"Glad we're safe in here. Sounds like quite the storm." Jack stretched out his long legs, leaned back, and took another sip of his beer.

Thunder rumbled in the distance, sounding amazingly like... *No, don't go there.*

"Did you get many customers today, or did the storm chase everyone away?" He looked at her like everything was normal. Like she wasn't fighting off panic.

"It... it was slow." She choked out the answer and tried to put on a nonchalant expression. Thunder crashed above them and she jumped.

"You okay?"

She nodded, hoping the storm ended soon, but the rain settled into a constant pounding on the roof.

She forced herself to relax and sipped on her beer.

"Want to eat out here by the fire?"

"Uh... how about the kitchen? It's nice and light in there." She couldn't think of any other plausible reason to give. She couldn't just say she wanted to be as far away from the fire as possible.

"Sure thing." He stood. "I'll just dish everything up and we'll eat."

"I'll help." Shooting one last dirty look at the fire, she fled into the kitchen.

Jack set the food on the table, and they took their seats. It was nice to have company at a meal again. She took a bite of the chili. "Oh, you were right. It's amazing."

"Thanks." He beamed at the compliment.

As they chatted and enjoyed their meal, she relaxed and was able to enjoy herself. "So, what did your Mom send over in the box she had for you?"

He laughed. "It turned out that there were three boxes. There were two afghans that she'd knitted herself. Brand new bath towels. Canned soup, boxed macaroni kits, every condiment known to mankind. Cleaning supplies. Oh, and a pair of binoculars of my dad's. She said I might like watching the birds on the beach. And a couple of framed family photos."

She leaned back in her chair. "Sounds like you made quite the haul."

"I did. I admit, those family photos and the afghans do make it feel more like home. The boxed macaroni kits? Not so much. She still thinks I'm eight." He shook his head, but his lips tilted into a slight smile that proved contagious.

Daisy smiled back at him, at their easy conversation, at the fact it was still dumping rain but the thunder and lightning had fled away into the distance. She stood. "Let me help you clean up."

"Okay," he agreed. "And I have some pieces of pie for us to have later if you like."

"I'd like." If she didn't watch out, she was going to put on twenty pounds after all this rich —and delicious—food she was having now. And she didn't have hiking and skiing to burn off the calories anymore.

Again with the Colorado comparisons.

She turned around and grabbed more dishes from the table, and Jack put the chili in the fridge. "More beer? Wine?"

"Wine might be nice. It's not like I'm driving." But she was pretty sure with his manners, he'd offer to walk her home.

"Go on in by the fire. I'll bring the wine and the pie."

Fine, she'd go sit by the fire, but she was going to ignore it. How she hated fireplaces now. It just reminded her of all those times...

Stop it.

Jack came in with the wine and pie and broke her thoughts. He turned on some low music, then sat beside her on the couch. "Sounds like it's going to rain all night."

"It kind of does. I thought this part of Florida was known for its hit-and-run storms. Blow in, blow out."

"Forecast says it's going to rain again tomorrow. But then it warms up and turns sunny again."

"That's good."

"I miss my morning runs." He took a sip of his wine. "Oh, this one is good. A slight woody flavor and maybe a hint of berry."

She took a sip. "Maybe blackberry?"

He nodded. "I think that's it."

They ate their pie and talked for a bit until she yawned. A traitorous yawn because she wasn't really ready to leave.

"I should walk you home." He set his glass down and stood. "You're tired. Or maybe bored." He winked at her.

"I'm not bored." She laughed. "I am a bit tired, though."

They nestled close together beneath her umbrella as he walked her back to her cottage. She opened her door and turned to him. "You should take my umbrella back with you. It's still pouring down rain."

"I'll be fine."

"If you're sure." She held it out to him one more time.

"Nope. But thank you. Good night. It was fun tonight."

"I had a good time, too."

He turned and raced across the distance to his cottage. He stopped on his porch and turned to wave to her. She waved back, then slipped inside her house and flipped on the lamp. The light spilled through the room as she gazed around her cottage with a critical eye.

She didn't have any family photos like Jack did. Or a hand-knitted afghan. Or really much that made the cottage feel like a home. Okay, she did have a vase of flowers she'd brought home from the shop that were just a little too spent to sell to a customer, but they still looked pretty. But there were no pictures on the wall. No knickknacks. The bookshelf had only a handful of books, standing lonely and empty against the wall.

She could blame the sparseness on the fact she hadn't been in town long, but she knew that wasn't it. But why had she been so resistant to making this cottage more homey? She should fix that. Decorate the cottage. Her *home*. It was really time to make this feel like home.

CHAPTER 11

E llen usually worked late on Wednesdays, so Daisy decided to ask Jack over for dinner. She was kind of getting used to having company to talk to over a meal. He seemed quite eager when he accepted her invite, which made her think he appreciated the mealtime companionship as much as she did. They both knew how challenging it could be to make friends in a new town. She searched online for simple, foolproof dinners and decided on a chicken dish that could be put in the slow-cooker before work. Not willing to attempt a fancy dessert, she picked up ice cream and chocolate sauce the night before and hoped Jack would like that.

Late Wednesday afternoon, she left work and hurried home, carrying a bouquet of fresh flowers, wishing she'd taken time to find a picture or two for her walls. Anything to make it not quite so barren and sparse. The flowers would have to do for now. She split them between two vases, one for the table and one out in the family room.

Looking around the room, she blanched at how lifeless and uninspired it looked. What would he think of her living here like this? One couch. One chair and a table lamp. One lamp by the door. She was more determined than ever to make an effort to decorate the place.

At least the chicken smelled delicious. She peeked into the crockpot. It looked good. Hopefully it tasted as good as it smelled and the chicken came out tender.

She went and freshened her makeup and ran a brush through her hair before deciding to pull one side back with a favorite silver clip. The woman staring back in the mirror surprised her. She stared critically. The last year or so had taken their toll, aged her. A smattering of wrinkles that she couldn't even say were laugh lines—she rarely laughed. A few strands of gray that thankfully were almost impossible to distinguish in her blonde hair. Her amber eyes stared back at her, accusing her of spilling way too many tears.

She twirled around, stopping the nonsense. A knock at the door saved her and she hurried to answer it.

"Hey," Jack said as he stood there smiling at her. "I hear this is the place to eat tonight."

"It is. Come in." She stepped back, and he entered the cottage. He ran his gaze around the room but thankfully didn't mention her spartan accommodations. "I'm making a new recipe. Chicken. Hope you like it."

"Smells wonderful." He followed her to the kitchen.

"Some wine before dinner?" She reached for a bottle of cabernet on the counter.

"Yes, please."

She poured them glasses and handed him one. Their fingers brushed with a moment of warmth, and she slowly pulled her hand back. "We could sit outside?"

"Sounds good. Been inside working all day."

They went outside, and she realized she needed nicer chairs out here, too. Comfortable ones that begged a person to sit down and relax. She'd just gotten two cheap metal ones because she worked such long hours. Who had much time to just… sit? But now she was embarrassed compared to the nice wicker ones that Jack had at his cottage. Although they'd been Mr. Cooper's, but that didn't make her feel less guilty.

And why was she being so critical of everything now? Judging her cottage, her looks. What did it matter? Had he even noticed the cheap chairs when he stopped by last week?

But it did matter to her. She wanted to feel like she belonged again. To feel like she was home. Didn't she?

Or did she? Because if you belonged somewhere and felt part of the place, if it all went away, it could devastate you.

"This is nice," Jack said as he stretched out his legs, oblivious to her bouncing thoughts.

"We've had glorious weather all week, haven't we?"

"No, I meant… having dinner with you again. I enjoy it."

Oh. She glanced over at him, then looked

down at her wine, concentrating on swirling it a few times in the glass.

"So, I was wondering…"

At his pause, she looked back up at him, and he leaned forward.

"I was wondering if I could take you out to dinner sometime."

"Like out somewhere, not at our homes?"

"Right…" He cleared his throat. "Like a… a date. Do you want to go out on a date with me?"

Was she ready for a date? Did she want to date someone? Wasn't just having neighborly dinners at each other's house enough?

"If not, that's okay," he added hurriedly.

"It's not that. It's just… it's been a while since I've dated."

"Bad breakup?" he asked.

How in the world did she answer that? She closed her eyes for a moment, fighting away the pain, fighting away the memories. "It was… abrupt. I wasn't expecting it." That was really a tiny white lie, now wasn't it? It didn't explain things at all. But… she wasn't up to explaining what really happened.

"Okay, if you're not ready to date. I get that.

How about we go out to dinner at Jimmy's? Just as friends. Really, I've gotten used to having company for meals. You know, other than my mom and her friends." He cocked his head to one side. "Would that work for you?"

"Yes, that would." She nodded. Going as friends would be fine. Actually, now that she'd had a moment to process, a date wasn't the worst idea she'd ever heard.

"How about Friday?"

"Friday works." She was opening the shop on Friday, and Ellen was scheduled to close.

"Meet you here at your place and we'll walk?"

"Yes, that works." She looked over at him. "And Jack..."

"Yep?"

"We can call it a date if you want to."

His eyes twinkled as he grinned. "Just trying to get out of paying for your meal, aren't you?"

"What? No." She shook her head quickly and frowned.

"Just teasing," he assured her.

She wasn't used to teasing these days. Though Kirk used to tease her relentlessly.

And then there he was. Standing on the

deck. Watching her. She blinked her eyes rapidly, assuring herself that Kirk wasn't actually here.

She jumped up, spilling her wine. "Oh." The red liquid spread across the boards of the deck. "I'll get something to clean that up."

She fled inside, her heart pounding. What was wrong with her? It had been almost two years now. Time enough to not fall apart every time his name popped into her head. And then the anger she'd tried so hard to fight back enveloped her.

None of it had to happen the way it did. It was his choice. And he hadn't chosen her.

Jack walked into the kitchen. "You okay?"

She swallowed and reached for the paper towels, struggling to compose herself, tamp down the anger, hide from the pain. "Sure. Yes."

Jack held out her glass. "At least it didn't break. Want me to pour you another?"

"Sure. I'll just go out and clean up my mess. Then I think we're about ready to eat." She fled back outside to sop up the spilled wine. Then she stood and took a few deep breaths, reciting the scientific names of flowers to help her calm down. Lilac—genus *Syringa*, family

Oleaceae. Tulip—genus *Tulipa*, family Liliaceae.

The door to the deck opened. "Need any help?"

"No. I've got it." She pasted on a smile and followed him back inside, assuring herself that she felt almost normal again. Almost.

Jack wasn't sure what had just happened, but Daisy had looked absolutely spooked for a moment there. A bit of terror etched on her features. Then she'd jumped up and spilled her wine.

Something had happened, he just wasn't sure what it was. Was it him asking her out on a date? He hoped not.

Daisy dished up their meal, smiling the whole time, but the smile didn't quite reach her eyes. Like she was trying to convince herself she was fine. She set the meal on the table and he sat down across from her.

He took one bite of the chicken and smiled. "This is great."

"Thanks. I was worried. A new recipe."

"Is that rosemary I taste in the sauce?"

She nodded and passed him a roll. "And I didn't bake these rolls. I got them from Sea Glass Cafe. I wasn't tempting fate by trying to make homemade rolls."

"Did you pick up cinnamon rolls at the same time?"

She laughed. "Not this time. I told myself I couldn't have them every single morning."

He shrugged. "I don't see why not. Seems like a perfectly reasonable plan to me. They're delicious."

"And fattening. Speaking of that... I picked up ice cream and chocolate sauce for dessert. Didn't want to push my luck with the whole making dinner thing. I haven't really cooked much in a long time."

"I love ice cream."

She looked relieved. "Good."

Now that they'd dissected their dinner choices, they sat in silence for a bit. She still seemed a bit jumpy or upset. He set down his fork. "Are you okay?"

"Yes, I'm fine." But her eyes betrayed her.

"You just seem a bit... distracted." No, she

seemed a bit upset, but he didn't want to put it that way.

"Really, I'm fine. Just a bit tired, I guess."

He still got the feeling she wasn't telling him the whole truth, but he gathered this was all he was getting for now.

After dinner, he helped her do the dishes, and they took their wine back out on the deck. He sat on the hard metal chair, wishing for the comfortable wicker chairs over at his place. Her cottage was fairly bare, but then she hadn't been here long and was busy getting her shop up and running. And she probably didn't have an interfering mother who sent over three boxes of things for her house.

Which reminded him. He didn't know much about her family. He turned to her. "So, do you have family nearby?"

She looked up quickly. "Ah… no."

"Where do they live?"

She looked down for a moment. "My parents are gone. Dad passed away when I was a child. Mom died about five years ago."

"I'm sorry."

"I have no siblings. I have an aunt, though. She… she lives in Colorado."

"Do you see her often?" It must be strange to just have one family member. He had his mother and brother, along with a handful of aunts and uncles and a dozen cousins. They got together every few years for big family reunions.

"Not often. I haven't seen her in a few years now."

It sounded like a lonely life to him. She hadn't made many friends here and didn't see her family. Well, she had one friend here. Him. And he was enjoying getting to know her. Liked her company. Their conversations. The way her eyes lit up when she talked about her shop.

She took the last sip of her wine. "I guess we should call it a night. I have an early morning."

"Of course." He swallowed the last of his wine and stood up, handing her the glass. He got the feeling she wanted the conversation about family to stop more than she really needed to end the evening. "Thanks for dinner. It was great. Loved it all. Especially the ice cream. Some of the best I've ever had."

"That was from the cafe, too. It really was good, wasn't it? It was their homemade vanilla."

"I'll have to remember that."

He climbed down the stairs. "I'll see you Friday, if not before."

"See you Friday."

He jogged over to his cottage, looking back before going inside. Daisy stood at the edge of her deck, looking out at the water. She was a quixotic mix of personalities. Funny, laughing, giving. But then a hint of sadness also hovered around her. He wasn't sure what that was about, but something had happened to her. He could feel it. Something that had affected her deeply.

Maybe he'd find out as he got to know her better. Or maybe it was one of those things a person liked to keep to themselves.

Daisy stood by the railing, watching the waves roll slowly to shore. Relentlessly. Never-ending. Just like her memories. She swore she saw Kirk again out of the corner of her eye.

"Go away. Leave me alone." She flung her arm wide. "Stop it." But of course, he wasn't there. But he always hovered around her, just out of sight. And nothing she did seemed to make him go completely away like she wanted.

She whirled around and headed inside, walking to the kitchen. She washed the wine glasses by hand, knowing they were perfectly fine to put in the dishwasher but needing something to do. To keep her busy. To keep Kirk's memory from popping back to haunt her.

Maybe she shouldn't have asked Jack to leave. They could have talked long into the night, and then she could have been tired enough to drop into a deep sleep. A sleep so deep that the nightmares wouldn't come and she wouldn't wake herself up screaming or crying.

She leaned against the counter, searching the room, looking for something to keep her occupied. Nothing out of place. Nothing to pick up or clean. With a sigh, she flicked off the kitchen light and headed toward her bedroom. The book she was reading was really good. Maybe she could get lost in it until she could barely keep her eyes open. That might work. Anything beat just hanging around dodging the memories.

She read until she couldn't keep her eyes open any longer and set the e-reader on the bed table. Soon, she was fast asleep.

But the nightmare came, as usual.

"Don't go," she pleaded with Kirk.

"I have to." He kissed her quickly.

"Please. Stay." She reached out and grabbed his hand.

"I can't. You know that. I have to go." He pulled his hand free, and with one last look at her, he slipped out the door.

The image was still etched into her mind. Taunting her in her dreams. The last time she'd seen him.

Then her dream flickered to the phone call.

She woke herself up with her screams.

CHAPTER 12

J ack went out for an early run the next
morning. He firmly believed there was
nothing like a good run to clear your head
at the start of the day. His feet pounded along
the hard-packed sand at the water's edge.
Beyond the mental benefits, running also helped
keep him in shape for his weekend job with the
beach rescue unit.

He'd done beach rescue and lifeguarding
for years, ever since he started during summer
breaks in college, and he really enjoyed it. Even
after he started his techie job, he kept certified
and up-to-date on his lifeguarding skills.
Luckily, he'd found positions that worked
around his regular job. But he had to stay in

good physical condition. Moonbeam's rescue unit shared a small gym with the beach lifeguards where he could lift weights or use the treadmills, but he preferred to run outside or swim when possible.

The extra job kept him busy here since he didn't know that many people and the unit needed the help. There was a lack of qualified applicants, so they were eager to take him on, even if he could only work weekend shifts. Most of the guys had been at the job for years. Quite a few were even older than he was.

Fifty. He was turning fifty this year. That was hard to believe. How did he get to that age? And while he was thinking that, why did his mother still think he was about ten?

He slowed down his pace to cool off and headed back toward his cottage. As he got close to Blue Heron Cottages, he saw Rose sitting out on the beach. He slowed some more and jogged up to her. "Morning, Rose."

"Good morning, Jack. I wondered when I'd see you out running again."

"Almost every day. Or a swim. Though the last few times I've gone the other direction, so I didn't see you."

"Do you like it? I've never been a runner. I do like a nice long beach walk, though."

"I do love running. The high it gives me. The way I feel after I finish. And I work for the beach rescue unit on the weekends, so I need to keep in shape."

"You do? That's fascinating. What an interesting job, I bet."

"It's a lot of sitting around sometimes. But we've rescued swimmers from riptides and they call us when boats are in distress. Things like that. I'm a certified lifeguard too, so I take on some of those shifts. There's a shortage of hires these days."

"That's your weekend job?"

"Yes, I'm a techie person during the week." He grinned. "Long hours inside at the computer. So the weekend job is a nice break from that. Though I've been known to take my computer outside on the deck and work from there. Remote work is the best thing to ever happen to my job."

"You sound like you're very busy."

He shrugged. "I am. But I've still been taking some time to just relax. I'm actually going on a date on Friday." *Now why was he telling*

Rose that? But she did have an aura about her that suggested a person could tell her anything.

"That's nice. Anyone I know?" Rose gave him a quick smile.

"Yes, Daisy."

"Oh, I hope you both have a nice time. She's such a nice lady."

"That she is." He nodded. "She's my next-door neighbor and we've had a few dinners together. I just thought it might be nice to actually have a date."

"I'm sure it will be."

"I haven't dated anyone since I moved here. My last girlfriend was—how do I say this nicely —fairly high maintenance and demanding. It exhausted me keeping up with Monique. Going to the events she thought she needed to be seen at. And she was critical of my choices, my clothes, my jobs. Hated that I worked as a lifeguard on the weekends. Said it was embarrassing to her." He shook his head. "I still don't know why I dated her so long. I guess because I knew breaking up would be a drama. And it was. Monique was furious when I told her I was moving here to Moonbeam."

"Doesn't sound like you two were a very

good fit."

"We weren't. But I was into the relationship too deep before I really realized it."

"Maybe you and Daisy will be a better fit."

"Maybe. I'm just glad to go out on a date with someone who is easy to be with and I can just be myself."

"It's always nice to be able to be yourself with someone, isn't it? I hope you both have a wonderful time."

"Thanks. I hope so, too." He glanced at his watch. "I better run. I've got a work call in twenty minutes."

"It was nice talking with you," Rose said.

"I'm sure I'll see you again soon on another run." He gave her a wave and jogged off toward his cottage, hoping to have a few minutes to grab a shower before his meeting.

Rose watched Jack jog down the beach. A nice young man. He'd be a good match for Daisy. They both seemed like hard-working, personable young people. Oh, she guessed they weren't that young. But younger than she was.

She couldn't imagine dating someone again. It seemed so foreign. The last time she dated someone before marrying Emmett would have been over fifty years ago. A long time.

She brushed off the cobwebs of the memory of her first date with Emmett. She'd been so nervous. She'd met him at the movie theater in town. There was no way he could show up at her house on his motorcycle. Her father would have had a tantrum.

Emmett was waiting for her at the entrance to the theater, two tickets in hand. He had on a clean, if worn, shirt and a pair of jeans that looked brand new. She'd always wondered if he'd bought them especially for their date but had never asked.

They'd gotten some popcorn and two sodas and took their seats near the far edge of the theater. She couldn't even remember the name of the movie. She could remember the brush of Emmett's hand when they both reached for the popcorn at the same time. The way she glanced at him a few times and saw that he was staring at her.

He walked her home after the movie. She stumbled slightly on the sidewalk and fell against him. He caught her in his arms. She still remembered his words. "I'll never let you fall."

And he hadn't. He'd been there for her from that day forward. For fifty years of marriage.

So how did someone take that life, that love, and put it aside and date someone new?

They didn't. That was her firm answer.

She couldn't imagine going out with someone new. She wouldn't even know how to act. Things were different now with those techie dating apps and online dating, and she didn't know what all these young people did to meet people.

But then she didn't need to meet anyone. She'd had a great love of her life. She didn't need to have a relationship with anyone else. Someone who was sure to pale in comparison to Emmett. He was the kindest, most wonderful man she'd ever met. She was content to live out the rest of her life alone. She still had a good life. She'd met wonderful friends here in Moonbeam. She was going to be okay.

She looked out over the water. "I miss you, my love."

She swore she heard him whisper, "You *will* be okay. I promise."

CHAPTER 13

Daisy opened Beach Blooms early that morning. There'd been no more sleep for her after the nightmares, so she drank a pot of coffee, finished two crossword puzzles, and once it was light, headed to work.

Ellen bustled into work mid-morning, grabbed her apron, and opened a shipment of ribbon. "You were right. This company makes beautiful ribbon." She held up a spool. "A perfect shade of teal."

"I ordered from them for my last shop," Daisy said.

Ellen looked up quickly. "You had a floral shop before this one? Where? Why didn't I know this?"

"Colorado." Why, oh why, was Colorado always just right in front of her face?

"I didn't know that. Why did you leave it and move here?"

And there was that question. Again. "I just… needed a change." And that, at least, was the truth. She'd desperately needed a change. Needed to get away.

"So, how was your date with Jack last night?"

Thankfully, Ellen moved on from Colorado. "It wasn't a date."

"Sure, whatever you say. Keep saying it."

"Well, I do have a date with him on Friday." The heat of a blush flushed her cheeks.

Ellen stopped unpacking the box and stared at her. "You do? That's great."

"We're going to Jimmy's for dinner."

"Perfect. I knew you'd eventually have to call one of your dinners a date." She grinned.

"Very funny."

"But seriously, he called it a date and everything?"

"He did."

"You'll need to leave work early tomorrow then and change and get ready."

"It's not that big of a deal. It's just dinner."

Ellen leaned her head to one side, eyeing her. "And when is the last time you had a date?"

"I… It was a very long time ago."

"Exactly what I thought. So you'll go home early tomorrow. Find a nice outfit to put on. Hopefully with a shirt that doesn't have Beach Blooms embroidered on it." Ellen rolled her eyes.

"I can manage that." She did have an outfit to wear. Probably. If she dug in the back of her closet.

"And do your makeup. Maybe curl your hair?" Ellen looked at her critically. "I bet your hair would look really cute with some beachy curls.

"I don't even know what that is."

"It's kind of like wavy curls. Loose ones. You should look on YouTube on how to do it. Your hair would look great that way."

"I don't know. I don't usually do much to my hair."

"I know, but a date calls for a little extra effort," Ellen insisted as she pulled out her phone and typed into it. She held it out for Daisy. "See, this is what they look like."

She scrolled through the pictures Ellen had pulled up on her phone. They did look nice. Not too fussy. "Okay, I might try it."

"Good." Ellen turned back to the box of ribbons, then paused. "And... try a hint of lipstick, too."

"So, what? You're like my dating coach now?"

"Let's just say I've had a ton of experience dating. Not that it has ever turned into a very serious relationship, but, wow, have I dated. So, you should listen to me. I give great advice." Ellen grinned.

Maybe she should take Ellen's advice because what did she know herself about dating? Little to nothing. It had been years. Now that Ellen had mentioned everything, she was starting to get even a little more nervous about the date. Just great. One more thing to worry about.

"I'll tell you what. I can bring my curling iron to work tomorrow. I'll do your hair before you leave for the day."

"I don't know..."

"Oh, come on. It will be fun. I love doing stuff like that. I'm always trying out new hairstyles. I've pretty much perfected the perfect beach wave."

She gave in. "Okay, we can try it. But if I don't like it, I'm going to run home and take a shower and start over."

"Fair deal." Ellen turned away but muttered under her breath, "But you're going to love it."

"I heard that." Daisy turned and went into the backroom to get another batch of flowers for the bouquets she was making.

All this talk about beach curls and what to wear and doing her makeup… Now she was nervous. *Very* nervous. Why couldn't life just be simple for once?

Ethan came in every day for a meal—if not two —which pleased Melody, but he hadn't asked her out on another date. And it had been almost a week since they'd talked and, she thought, sorted this all out. He had come by a few evenings to walk her home from work but never asked her out.

This wasn't really what she'd consider slowing down their dating relationship… it was more like halting it. If he didn't ask her out soon, she might just ask him. Maybe. But she was just old-fashioned enough, or uncertain enough of the whole dating thing, that she wanted him to ask.

How in the world did people get into dating these days? With dating apps? She couldn't imagine doing that, though she knew plenty of people who had met their Mr. or Mrs. Right that way. She just wasn't interested in meeting some guy that way. She hadn't even thought she was interested in dating... until Ethan asked her out.

The door to the cafe opened and there he was. Coming in for a late lunch. Her heart did a little skip, which she ignored, of course.

He walked over and sat at a table, and she hurried to finish up with her customer and go wait on him.

"Hey, Mel," he said as she walked up to him.

"Hi. I hope you're hungry. Evelyn made her meatloaf today. It's excellent. I bet we sell out of it before dinner is over tonight."

"Meatloaf it is, then." He looked up at her, easing into a smile. "I don't suppose you could join me?"

She looked around the cafe. Three more tables of customers still eating their meals, but there was one other waitress working. "I probably could. Unless a big table comes in."

She headed back to the kitchen to turn in the order. "Evelyn, I'm going to take a break and have some lunch with Ethan."

"Sounds good. I know you're working until closing tonight."

"Two meatloaf lunches." She grinned at Evelyn. "Can't resist your meatloaf. And I'll go check out my last table, then come get our food."

She rang out a table of four, gave Ethan a large sweet tea, and headed to get their meals. She carried them out and sank onto the chair across from Ethan, scooting his plate across the table.

He reached for it and adjusted it in front of him. After a bite, he let out a little sigh of satisfaction. "Her meatloaf is the best, isn't it?"

"It is."

"You working late tonight?"

"I am. Closing."

"I could come by and walk you home."

"If you'd like." *Or, you could, you know… ask me out…*

They talked about the weather. The Jenkins twins' latest gossip. A big fundraiser at The Cabot Hotel coming up. Just regular daily chatter.

Maybe she should break down and ask *him* out.

"Ethan—"

"Melody—"

They spoke in the same split second.

"You go ahead." She nodded at Ethan.

"Okay." He leaned back in his chair, then sat forward again, resting his forearms on the table. "I heard that Misty Hartman is singing at The Lucky Duck over on Belle Island this weekend. Friday, Saturday, and Sunday night. Would you like to go out with me and go hear her?"

"Oh, I love her singing. She has a lovely voice." He'd finally asked her out. She wanted to jump up from her seat and twirl around. She could feel a dopey smile lift the corners of her mouth.

He eyed her. "So that's a yes?"

"Yes, I'd love to." Her heart soared with the fact he was finally, *finally*, asking her out again.

"Which night works best for you?"

"Sunday would. Emily is working and two other servers. They'll be fine without me."

"Perfect." His eyes sparkled in anticipation. "It will be great. I'm glad you said yes."

"Of course I said yes." Hadn't they hammered this all out last week? That she was more than willing to date him?

He grinned sheepishly. "I was just worried if I asked you out too soon that you'd say no."

She shook her head. "We need to figure this whole dating thing out, don't we?"

He laughed gently. "I guess we do."

She stood. "I should get back to work."

He rose, dropping some bills on the table for his meal. "I'll see you tonight after work, though, right? To walk you home?"

"Yes, I'll see you tonight."

She grabbed the dishes and headed back to the kitchen.

Evelyn walked over as Melody set the dishes on the growing stack by the dishwasher. "You look happy."

"I am. I'm going on a date with Ethan on Sunday. We're going over to The Lucky Duck."

"Oh, Misty is back in town, I heard. She's singing there this weekend."

"She is."

"I hope you have a lovely time."

"I was just happy he finally asked me out again. I thought I'd scared him off." She laughed.

"He's a bit of a shy one, that Ethan. But he knows what he wants."

"What do you mean by that?"

"He likes you, Melody. He *wants* you. It's been obvious for a very long time. The guy is totally smitten."

Melody turned and started rinsing the dishes and putting them in the dishwasher. Was he smitten? Smitten, what a funny word. But she liked it. She wouldn't mind a bit if Ethan was smitten with her.

CHAPTER 14

As Daisy got ready on Friday, she had to admit she liked the loose curls Ellen had made in her hair. Just a bit fancier than her usual, but not fussy. She'd also found a simple dress in the back of her closet in a nice shade of buttercream yellow. She didn't own a pair of heels, so she found some teal flats to wear. Then she redid her makeup and obeyed Ellen's suggestion to put on a touch of lipstick.

She looked in the mirror, barely recognizing herself. All this hubbub for a simple date on the wharf. And yet, she did want to look different. Special. There was a look in her eyes that she hadn't seen in a very long time. Excitement.

Anticipation. No hint of sadness. It was a very welcome change.

She gently touched the beach waves and smiled. Yes, she liked this look.

Jack knocked, and she hurried to answer the door. His hair was still damp from a recent shower, a blue polo shirt stretched across his broad chest, and khaki slacks covered his long legs.

"You look great," he said, running his gaze over her. "I mean, you always look nice. You just look… really amazing." He smiled sheepishly. "I'm probably making a mess of my words. Anyway, you look very pretty tonight."

"Thank you. You do, too. I mean, not pretty… handsome." She blushed.

He chuckled, his eyes sparkling with amusement. "We're doing really great at this date thing, aren't we?"

"We could start over," she suggested.

"Great idea." He whirled around and walked out the door, pulling it shut behind him. In a moment, she heard his knock again.

Laughing, she opened the door. "Why hello."

"Hi. You look smashing tonight." He winked.

"You look rather dapper yourself." The tension between them disintegrated into tiny grains of sand.

"You ready to go?"

"I am."

They headed out and walked slowly down the sidewalk toward the wharf. Their steps fell into a rhythm as they strolled along in the early evening light. A light breeze blew her hair about her shoulders, and she hoped her beachy curls were holding their own.

Twinkling lights strung across the walkway between the shops and restaurants welcomed them to the wharf. The first time she came to the wharf, she'd been enchanted by the lights and the way they softly illuminated the walkway. It still did enchant her a bit. Especially with Jack walking by her side.

Now, where had that thought come from? She was just going out on a simple date. You know, a *simple* date where she'd spent way too much time and angst getting ready.

Walker Bodine greeted them as they entered

Jimmy's. "Good evening. Great to see you two again."

"Hi, Walker." Jack stretched out his hand and they shook. "Hoping for a table right by the water."

"We can do that. Follow me."

They followed Walker to a high-top table by the railing, and Jack pulled out the chair for her. She climbed up onto it and he sat down across from her.

Walker handed them menus. "Special tonight is the grouper basket. Fried grouper. Hushpuppies. Coleslaw. Oh, and a slice of key lime pie for dessert."

Didn't take much to convince her that she was getting the special.

"I'll send Aspen over to get your order."

"Thanks, Walker." She picked up her menu but was still fairly certain nothing would beat the special tonight. Her mouth watered just thinking about it.

Jack picked up his menu. "You want wine tonight? Or what would you like to drink?"

"I think a beer sounds good. I've tried the local craft beer they carry. It was really good."

Aspen came over to their table carrying two

glasses of water. "Hi. Can I get your drink order?"

"We'll both have the local craft beer," Jack ordered.

"Good choice. I'll be right back with them."

Daisy perused the menu, then set it down. Nothing sounded as good as the special. "I'm going to have the grouper special."

He set his menu down, too. "I'm going to have it, too. Love the grouper here."

Aspen brought back two beers in chilled glasses. "Here you go."

Jack handed Aspen their menus. "We'll both have the special."

"Another good choice." Aspen took the menus. "Won't be too long." She headed over to a nearby computer station and entered their orders. Walker came up to her and pressed a quick kiss on her forehead. Her eyes lit up, and she laughed, jokingly pushing him away. "Don't let my boss see you do that. I'm on the clock."

Daisy smiled at the two of them. "Walker and Aspen make a cute couple, don't they?" She nodded her head their direction.

"So, in your definition, what makes a cute couple?" Jack's eyes twinkled.

"I don't know. I just like the way he looks at her. How quickly she smiles at him. Just… like they fit."

He nodded. "Okay, I get that."

"The Jenkins twins were in my shop the other day. They mentioned that Walker and Aspen have been dating since she came to town."

"The Jenkins twins?" Jack's eyebrows rose.

"Jackie and Jillian Jenkins. They're the bearer of all news in Moonbeam. Always seem to know what's going on with everyone." She laughed. "And they aren't afraid to share their news.

"I haven't met them yet."

She looked up and grinned. "Oh, well. What a coincidence. You're in for a treat. They're headed our way."

The twins stopped and said something to Walker and Aspen, then headed toward them. "Well, Daisy. Good evening."

"Hi." She couldn't tell them apart, so she just gave them a generic hello.

"So, you're dating Mona's son," the other twin said.

"Hi, I'm Jack." He smiled at the ladies.

"Otherwise known in Moonbeam as Mona's son."

"We didn't know you two were dating, did we, Jackie?" Jillian said more than asked.

"No, we didn't. But now we do." Jackie bobbed her head. "Good to see two young people find each other."

"It's just one date," Daisy protested. And she wouldn't exactly consider the both of them young.

"Hopefully, there'll be lots more." Jillian eyed them both, then took Jackie's arm. "We should go to our table now. Nice seeing you two."

"Nice meeting you," Jack said as the two women walked away.

"And that was a Jenkins twin interrogation. We'll be the talk of the town by tomorrow."

Jack looked a bit shocked. "Really?"

"Really." She nodded. "Hope that's okay with you."

"I guess it's fine." He leaned back in his chair and took a sip of his beer. "I'm just not quite used to living in a small town where everyone knows your business."

"That's small towns for you. But I love small

towns. You actually know people all around you. And Moonbeam has all these wonderful festivals. And neighbors help each other out."

"Hey, you've got a great neighbor now. Hopefully he'll be helpful." He winked.

She loved how he winked at her when he was teasing. Kind of an inside secret connection with him. "Hopefully my neighbor will be helpful." She smothered a smile. Helpful and handsome. What more could she want out of a neighbor?

And he really was handsome. His dark brown hair had just a hint of gray at the temple. His brown eyes changed from caramel to a copper color as he looked out at the bay and the last of the sun's rays illuminated his features. When he teased her, slight laugh lines hovered at the corners of his eyes. She realized she was staring at him while listing off his attractive qualities in her mind and turned her attention to the rivulets of water sliding down the outside of her beer glass. She picked it up and took a sip, hoping he hadn't noticed.

Thankfully, Aspen delivered their orders just then. "Need anything else? I brought you some drawn butter with the specials. That's my favorite for dipping the grouper and the hushpuppies in."

"Thank you." She looked at the basket in front of her. Crispy grouper, golden hushpuppies, and a dish of coleslaw. "It smells delicious."

"I'll bring your key lime pie when you finish." As Aspen walked away, she stopped and said something to Walker, who was now working behind the bar. The man did everything here at the restaurant, it seemed. Walker said something back, and she blushed.

Yes, they were a cute couple.

Daisy turned her attention back to her meal and Jack. But *not* staring at him.

"This is great." Jack waved a bite of grouper on his fork. "I don't know how they do it, but it's the best grouper I've had."

"It's really good." She dipped a bite in the butter and the crispy fish with the warm butter just melted in her mouth. Delicious.

As they ate, the sun put on a show for them with brilliant oranges and purples splashed across the sky and reflecting on the harbor.

"Did you plan that just for our date?" She pointed out at the fabulous sunset.

"Of course. Ordered it up special." His lips twitched in a smile, and those laugh lines she'd admired etched the corners of his eyes. "I'm powerful like that."

After they finished their meals, Aspen brought their pie. The tart taste of the pie was the perfect complement to their meal. They lingered over dessert, then Jack paid the bill and stood. "Ready?"

"Yes. And thank you. The meal was wonderful."

"The company was too." He tossed an easy smile her way.

He made her feel so comfortable and yet... a bit on edge, too. Excited maybe. Anyway, it had been a wonderful meal, and she was glad her first foray into dating again was going so well.

He took her elbow and led her out of the restaurant and down the wharf. The wind had picked up and now she was certain her beach curls were a disaster, but there wasn't much she could do about it.

They ambled along the streets, weaving in and out of the light from the lampposts until they reached their cottages. Jack paused on the sidewalk between their homes.

"Would you like to come in for a drink?" He glanced at his watch. "It's not too late yet."

"Yes, that sounds nice." She wasn't ready to call the night finished. A drink would be a pleasant way to delay the end of the date, something she found herself not looking forward to.

CHAPTER 15

Jack unlocked his door and Daisy followed him into his cottage as he flipped on a lamp. "I'll just go get us something to drink. Red wine?" Luckily he'd picked up a few bottles the other day at the grocery store.

"Perfect." Her soft footsteps echoed as she followed him into the kitchen.

His breakfast dishes were sitting in the sink, and a box of cereal was on the counter. He should have taken time to clean up the mess. He grabbed the cereal box and shoved it into the pantry.

He chose a bottle of wine, and it gave up a vigorous pop as he opened it. He poured two glasses and handed one to Daisy. "Want to sit outside? The wind is coming from the front of the house, so we should be pretty much protected out on the deck."

He switched on a solar lantern on a table on the deck. They settled on a wicker loveseat with generous cushions, sitting side by side. Daisy turned slightly toward him, and he tried not to stare at her lips as she took a few sips. He quickly looked down at his own glass, concentrating on the burgundy-colored liquid.

But then he couldn't help himself and glanced over at her again. She had waves in her hair tonight and they lightly framed her face. He really liked the look. He wondered if she'd done that just for him. Just for the date. He hadn't seen her hair look that way before. But going out on a date with him probably wasn't much of a big deal. She probably had lots of dates. And why not? She was a successful businesswoman and fun to be with and, as an added bonus, really pretty.

As if she could read his thoughts, she finger-combed her waves before glancing up at him, a smile playing at her lips. "Ellen did the curls in my hair tonight. I'm not used to them."

"They look nice." *You look nice. Beautiful. Pretty.*

But he didn't say those words. This was all so unexpected for him. He'd about sworn off women after his fiasco with Monique. But Daisy was different. Easy to be with. She accepted him just like he was. He didn't feel like he needed to warp into a different person for her.

Daisy yawned and smiled again. "I'm so relaxed now. Your place is cozy. I want to get more things for my cottage and make it feel more like home. And your deck furniture is so comfortable. Better than my metal chairs."

"Thanks. I admit my mom's boxes full of items did make this place seem more like mine. But these great chairs are all Mr. Cooper's."

"I want pictures for the walls and a few more pieces of furniture. I think I might hit up some thrift shops or secondhand stores. I love shopping at places like that. Of course, I'd have to find time to do that."

"But it will be fun, won't it? To decorate your home?"

"I think so. I'm tired of it being so plain."

"If you need someone to wrestle your furniture around, I'm your man."

"I'll remember that. Might take you up on the offer. Looks like you are going to be a helpful neighbor." Her eyes sparkled in the light of the lantern.

She set her wineglass on the table beside her and leaned back in the chair, precariously close to him, their shoulders touching now. She looked up at him with a contented smile. "This is nice." She turned and looked out at the sea, which was good, because it was dangerously easy to get lost in her eyes.

They both looked out at the water as the waves rolled to shore, their frothy tips captured in the moonlight. He wasn't sure how long they sat in silence until her head gently came to rest on his shoulder. He glanced down at her. She was fast asleep.

He slipped his arm around her shoulder, trying to make her more comfortable. A tiny sigh escaped her lips. A sigh that ignited a flame, racing through his veins. But he ignored it. Kind of. The lantern illuminated her face, so relaxed in sleep. He wanted to touch her cheek. Run his finger along her jawline. He settled on reaching over and gently pushing back a lock of her hair that had fallen across her face.

Right now, in this moment, he couldn't

imagine being anywhere else. Daisy had captivated him. Enchanted him. So unexpected, but so… appreciated. A surprise he wasn't prepared for here in Moonbeam. He so wanted to lean down and kiss her forehead. No, what he really wanted was for her to wake up so he could kiss those lovely pink lips of hers. The ones that had held him entranced when she sipped her wine.

Eventually, his arm started to tingle, but there was no way he would move and disturb her. She shifted slightly, and a frown crossed her face. She moved again. He gently covered her hand, resting on his leg. She jerked her hand away and shifted again.

"No. No. Please," she murmured.

Should he wake her?

"Don't go." Her muscles twitched.

He couldn't bear watching her struggle in her dreams.

"No." It was more a scream this time, and she sat up straight, eyes opened, dazed.

"Hey, you're okay." He wanted to reach out and take her in his arms, comfort her. But he wasn't even sure she realized she'd been having a bad dream.

She looked around her, shoving her hair back as her eyes cleared. "Oh, I fell asleep."

"You did."

"I'm sorry. I can't believe I fell asleep like that." She shook her head, her waves bobbing around her shoulders.

"I didn't mind." At all. In fact, he'd enjoyed it. It had been... peaceful.

She rubbed her hand over her face. "I guess I should go home. Sorry I wasn't better company."

"You were perfect company. I had a great evening."

She rose from the seat, and coolness immediately hovered by his side. The side where she'd just moments earlier rested against him. He stood. "I'll walk you home."

They trudged across the sand between their cottages and up the steps on her deck.

"Thank you. I had a nice time. And really, I'm embarrassed I fell asleep like that."

"Don't worry about it. I had a great evening."

She opened the door and stood in the doorway, looking fully recovered from her bad dream. The moonlight spilled around her, enchanting him once again.

He sucked in a deep breath, taking his chances. "I know it's only our first date—if you don't count all the meals we had before tonight —but would you mind if I kissed you good night?"

She paused for the slightest moment, her eyes widening. "I… uh… I wouldn't mind."

Right answer. He leaned in and kissed her gently on those lips he'd been staring at all night, one hand gently wrapping around the nape of her neck. Then he reluctantly pulled away.

He carefully studied her face, watching for her reaction. A bemused smile played at the corners of her lips and her eyes locked with his.

"That was unexpected," she whispered. "But very nice."

"You've been unexpected, Daisy. I didn't think I'd meet someone like you." He took one of her hands in his, and immediately electricity shot through him. "I enjoy spending time with you."

"I like spending time with you, too."

"So, we'll do this again? Go out on another date?"

"I'd like that."

"And how about one more good-night kiss? Just to make sure I'm doing it right." He grinned at her.

She laughed. "Just to make sure."

And he kissed her again, longer this time. Her hands rested against his chest, searing him. He put his hands on her waist, resisting the urge —just barely—to pull her tightly against him. She finally pulled back, her cheeks flushed. "I'm pretty sure you're doing it right."

He grinned again. "Maybe we'll just have to keep trying on our next date. To be absolutely certain."

"Of course, we have to be certain." She gave him one more long look—a look that placed him firmly under her spell—and slipped inside.

He headed across the sand now, feeling alone but elated. He got halfway back to his cottage before he realized he hadn't actually asked her out again. He'd correct that the next time he saw her. He couldn't wait for a second date. And another kiss.

Daisy walked into her cottage and sank onto the sofa, reaching her hand up to touch her lips. How long had it been since someone had kissed her? She knew exactly how long it had been. The exact day. Her thoughts warred with her, but she pushed them away.

Jack. Jack was an unexpected blessing with this move to Moonbeam. She wasn't looking to date someone, but here he was. Here she was.

She'd had such a good time tonight. It was relaxing and exciting at the same time.

But then there was that dream. Kirk. The dream she couldn't hide from. The one that repeated almost nightly. Had she screamed out loud or only in her dream? Jack would have said something if she had, wouldn't he?

How could she have fallen asleep like that? But it had been so relaxing sitting there with him.

Until it hadn't.

But then he'd walked her home and kissed her. The heat of his lips still lingered on hers. The feel of his heart beating beneath her hand.

How had all this happened? And so quickly?

She'd only known him a couple of weeks. Was she ready for this? For a relationship with someone? Or was this really a relationship? It was one date and two kisses. That wasn't really a relationship, was it?

No, of course not. It was just dating. And yet her heart fluttered as she remembered his kiss. And she wanted to go out with him again. Kiss him again.

And yes, she wanted to have a relationship with him. She missed that. Having a special someone. Someone she could be herself around and talk to and just... be with.

The other side of her warned her, though. *If you get serious with someone, you're risking getting hurt again.*

She just didn't know which side of herself to listen to...

CHAPTER 16

Jack headed over to his mother's for dinner after his shift on Saturday. She'd been asking him to dinner all week, but he'd been busy. Busy mostly with Daisy. He wanted to ask her out again. He should call her and do that. Maybe he'd do it tonight if it wasn't too late when he got home.

Then he laughed at the thought. His mother never stayed up late. He'd be back early.

He knocked on the door and went in when he heard her call to come in.

She was in the kitchen, an apron on, frying chicken at the stove. She looked up at him accusingly. "Jackson, I hear you've been dating Daisy."

"Hi, Mom. Good to see you, too."

She stood there, waiting, spatula in hand.

He sighed. "How did you hear that?"

"The Jenkins twins."

"Ah, yes. Saw them at Jimmy's last night."

"Why didn't you tell me you were dating her?"

"It was one date, Mom. One date. It's not like it's anything serious." He'd had a great time, though—not that he was going to tell his mother that. She already knew way too much about his life since he'd moved to Moonbeam. The memory of kissing Daisy poked at him, but he ignored it and headed to the fridge to pull out a beer.

"Did you have a good time?" She wasn't going to let this go.

"I did."

"Did she?" His mother sent him a questioning glance before turning back to the chicken.

"I guess so."

"Did you ask her out again?"

"I haven't yet, Mom. The date was only yesterday."

"But if you had a good time, you should.

She's a nice woman. I enjoyed getting to know her when we saw her at Jimmy's." She turned back toward him. "And you should take her somewhere other than Jimmy's. You've been there twice with her now. Expand your horizons."

"I like Jimmy's," He quickly defended his choice.

"It's a wonderful restaurant. I love going there. But maybe you could take her somewhere more… romantic."

"Who said anything about romance?"

She shrugged. "Never hurts to woo a woman a little bit."

Woo a woman. That was one way to put it. He did want to go out with Daisy again. Kiss her again. Spend time with her. He glanced at his watch. Yes, hopefully later this evening he could talk to her and ask her out on another date.

And hopefully their second date would be free of any bad dreams. There'd been a bit of sadness and even fright in her eyes when she woke up. And that scream of hers? It tore at his heart. But she'd recovered quickly. Still, he'd like to know what haunted her so much to have a dream like that.

He'd like to chase whatever it was far away from her. The protective urge surprised him. Ignoring it, he leaned against the counter, twisted the cap off the beer, and took a swig.

"Glasses are in the cabinet." His mother pointed with a lift of her chin.

He wanted to say the bottle was fine but knew she liked him to use a glass. He retrieved a tall glass from the cabinet and poured the amber liquid into it. "Want me to set the table, Mom?"

"That would be nice. Don't forget the placemats." She pointed to a drawer.

He set the table while she finished making the meal. Fried chicken. One of his favorites. But of course. His mother was always making his favorites because she was positive he wasn't eating enough. She might be all in his business and ask way too many questions, but he adored her. The best mom ever.

He walked over and kissed her cheek. "Thanks for making me dinner."

"Of course. I love cooking for you. Now go sit down and I'll dish everything up."

He enjoyed dinner with his mom, then

helped her with the dishes. She'd continued with the personal questions, of course, in spite of his best efforts to steer her off course. Then she loaded him up with leftovers—enough for a week of meals. He kissed her goodbye and then glanced at his watch as he was leaving. Just eight o'clock. Still early enough. He'd call Daisy as soon as he got home.

Daisy sat out on her deck, sipping a cup of chamomile tea. A lovely way to end a busy day of work. Too bad she still didn't have any comfortable chairs. She vowed to go shopping for some next week.

The lights came on in Jack's cottage—not that she'd been watching for them. He stepped out onto his deck and turned toward her house. When he saw her sitting there, he waved. She waved back, motioning for him to come over.

If he wanted to…

She smiled when he bounded down his steps and strode across the sand toward her. He climbed onto the deck. "Hey there," he said as he lounged against the railing.

"Hi. I was just enjoying some tea. Want some?"

"No, I'm good. Just got back from dinner at Mom's. Fried chicken, mashed potatoes, homemade rolls, green beans. I swear she thinks I'm a starving, growing teenager, so she needs to feed me constantly."

"Sounds delicious."

"It was. And I do appreciate it. I enjoy being here, and now I'm able to spend time with her. She just..." He shrugged. "She asks a lot of questions."

"I think that's what moms do. She just cares about you." Not that she'd really know. It wasn't like her mom had been very typical.

"I know. It's just an adjustment with the constant questions and her knowing so much about my day-to-day life now." He broke into a grin. "Oh, and you were right. The Jenkins twins spread the word about our date. Mom questioned me endlessly."

"Told you. Once the twins know something, everyone knows it. You okay with everyone knowing we're dating?" Well, they'd had one date. That didn't actually mean they were dating, did it?

"I'm absolutely fine with it." He nodded vigorously, then pushed off the railing and walked over to her. Smiling down at her, he held out a hand. She took it, and he pulled her gently to her feet. Her heart fluttered as she stood right next to him.

"And I'd like to kiss you again if that's okay. I've been thinking about kissing you all day."

And she'd been thinking about kissing him. She nodded, and he leaned in and kissed her, taking his time, his strong hands resting on her shoulders. Which was a good thing because his kiss made her world spin out of control as she got lost in it.

He finally pulled away, and she rested her hands on his hips, steadying herself.

"I could do that all day. All night." He gave her that wink that made her feel so connected to him.

"Then maybe you should do it again." The words just slipped out.

And he did. And again.

Finally, she pulled away, laughing. "We can't really stand here all night kissing, can we?" Though she kind of wanted to. More than kind of.

"Probably not." A regretful look covered his features. "I do have to get up early for work."

"Working on a Sunday?" She thought his job was more of a weekday nine-to-five type job.

"Oh, it's my second job."

"I didn't know you had a second job."

"I do. I work for the beach rescue unit."

The world paused as his words sank in. *Rescue unit.* Did he say rescue unit? Her hand flew involuntarily to cover her heart. "You what?"

"The rescue crew. I take shifts on the weekends. I've been doing it for years in different areas."

"Rescue?" She could barely get the word out.

"Yes, things like rescuing boats in distress, swimmers from riptides. And checking the coastline after tropical storms come through. Things like that. The county just started up a jet ski rescue team and we run a few rescue boats."

Her heart pounded in her chest, and she struggled to breathe. Rescue work. He did dangerous rescue work.

He looked questioningly at her. "Are you okay?"

"Fine." One-word answer. And she was doing good to get that out.

"Anyway, I've got an early shift tomorrow. But I was wondering. About that next date…"

"No." She stepped back, putting more distance between them. Distance she needed. Craved.

He frowned. "No? You have a busy work week? I was going to see if you wanted to go out later this week. Mom said I should take you somewhere more romantic."

She shook her head. "No. I don't think that's a good idea."

"So you're busy?" His brow furrowed.

"No… it's not that. I just—" She couldn't even begin to explain to him why dating him was the last thing in the world she wanted. The last thing she wanted after hearing he worked rescue.

"Why not? I thought… Weren't we just kissing? It was good, right?" He stared straight into her eyes. The eyes that begged her to admit she'd felt something with his kisses. "I felt the connection with you. I know you felt something, too."

And she had. But she was going to forget those feelings. Ignore them until they went far, far away.

"I... I changed my mind. I'm not ready to date someone." Sounded lame, but it would have to do. Her hands shook, and she balled them into fists.

"But I thought—"

"No. I'm sorry. No. You should go. Please go." She whirled around and fled into the house, leaving him standing there looking stunned. But she didn't care. She would not date a guy with a dangerous job. Too risky to care about someone who put their life on the line like that. She'd learned her lesson—*twice*—and didn't need to be taught it again.

CHAPTER 17

W*hat just happened?* Jack stared at where Daisy disappeared into her cottage like she was just a mirage. A mirage like those kisses? Good kisses. And he knew she felt something. He knew it.

But then... she'd just shut down. Pulled away. And he swore there was fear in her eyes. But why? Why had she changed her mind? She was hot... and then icy cold. It didn't make sense.

He trudged down the stairs and turned back to look at the empty deck. Confusion raced through him. Something had spooked her. But what? He ran through their conversation. He'd told her that he had a second job, but she worked long hours. It couldn't be that.

He raked his fingers through his hair, unable to leave. He halfway wanted to bound up those stairs and bang on her door and ask her to come out and talk to him. But she'd told him to leave.

And she'd been really, *really* definite in her answer to going on another date. No.

No. No. No.

But why? They'd been getting along so well. What had he done? He slowly turned and plodded across the sand to his cottage. The distance loomed now instead of feeling like a quick little jump between their places.

He went inside and flicked on a lamp, looking around the cottage. Even with everything his mother had given him, the emptiness and coldness mocked him. He headed to the kitchen and snagged a beer from the fridge, taking a long swallow of the cool liquid. He wiped his hand across his mouth. The mouth that had just been kissing Daisy. Kissing her before she pulled away and shut down on him. Told him to leave.

He went out onto the deck and hoped the cool breeze would calm his jangled emotions.

Women were so hard to figure out. Just when you thought you knew them, they changed.

At first, Monique had been everything he thought he wanted in a woman. Then she became impossible and judgmental.

And then he was beginning to think Daisy was the perfect match. Easy to be with. Fun. And he had to admit his heart thumped like a teenaged boy with a crush when he saw her. He'd thought that maybe this time things would work out. That maybe Daisy was everything he wanted and needed in a woman.

He drained the beer and headed inside. He should have listened to himself when he swore off dating.

She should have listened to the smarter side of herself that warned her to stay away from Jack. But no, she'd foolishly jumped in before she really knew him. She stared down at her shaking hands, willing them to steady, but they'd have nothing of it.

She'd left her teacup outside, but no way she was going out to retrieve it. It could wait until morning. When she was sure Jack was nowhere in sight.

How could she have fallen for a man who did rescue work? Put his life in danger? She thought he was a nice, safe, techie guy.

There was no way they could be involved now. And her heart crumbled a bit at the surety of that knowledge.

His kisses had set her heart soaring, and she'd been so happy—was it really just a handful of minutes ago? She'd been looking forward to another date with him.

But now it was impossible.

If she'd learned anything from her time with Kirk, it was imperative that she protect her heart. She couldn't go through a loss like that again.

She closed her eyes, chasing away the memories. The sound of the avalanche. The endless hours of hope and waiting. And more waiting.

She would not do that again.

When she first found out Kirk worked ski patrol, she'd been leery of dating him. After all, hadn't she lost her police officer dad when she was just in grade school? That should have been lesson one.

But Kirk wooed her, and she couldn't resist his smile. She finally gave in. For three years they dated, and when he proposed to her, she said yes.

Proposed just a week before he chose his job over her. She was engaged for a mere seven days...

Tears rolled down her cheeks in hot trails of anger. How could life do this to her again? First her dad. Then Kirk. So why had the universe thrown Jack into her path? Why had she fallen for him?

Because she had. She cared about him. But she'd fix that. She'd only known him a few weeks. How hard could he be to get over?

She dashed her hand across her face, wiping the tears away.

Next time, she'd listen to the side of her that warned her to stay away. To protect her heart. No more foolishly falling for someone. The next man she went out with, she'd make sure she knew all the jobs he did. Not that she thought she'd date again. It was too risky. Too hard. Too painful.

She just couldn't put herself through it again. That was too much heartache for one person to bear.

Now she wished she hadn't helped him find Mr. Cooper's cottage. It was going to be awkward with him living right next door. A long sigh surged through her body.

It wasn't fair. Life wasn't fair.

And how many times had she said that in the last few years?

Well, she had her shop, and she'd just throw herself into work. That would help. She'd keep so busy she had no time for her memories of Kirk, and no time for the if-onlys about Jack.

CHAPTER 18

M elody and Ethan walked into The Lucky Duck about seven Sunday night. Willie Layton, the owner, was working behind the bar. He gave them a wide, welcoming smile and motioned for them to take a table. The place was crowded, but they found a table near the stage. Ethan took a seat beside her, facing the stage.

A server bustled over to their table with a pen and an order pad. "Got here just in time. Misty is about ready to start. You here for food? Drinks?"

"I'll have a burger and one of Willie's famous basil motonics." Melody loved the burgers here, and Willie's drink was amazing.

"Same for me," Ethan said.

"Fries, coleslaw, or hushpuppies?"

"Fries for me."

"Me too." Ethan nodded.

"Be back with your drinks in a flash."

The last tables filled up and the bar area grew crowded. "Looks like Misty is a big draw for The Lucky Duck." Melody ran her gaze around the room. The last time she was here, the place had been busy, but not crowded like this.

"She's a talented singer. I'm not surprised. Heard she had some gig in Nashville and that's why she hasn't played here in a while. She's back here visiting family."

Misty sat down, said hello into the microphone, and the crowd quieted. "Glad you all came out tonight. Good to see old friends and new ones." She nodded to a table right near her. "And that's my momma. She's been here all three nights to hear me sing."

"I've missed hearing you sing. You were away too long." Her mom's voice could be heard across the low murmur of the crowd.

"My biggest fan." Misty grinned as she

started strumming her guitar and started into a slow ballad.

Their server delivered their drinks, and Melody took a sip. Willie's basil motonic really was an interesting, refreshing drink.

Ethan leaned back in his chair and draped his arm around her shoulders. She liked that. There was an ease between them tonight. Like when they'd just been friends, before the awkwardness of dating. She leaned a bit closer to him and he smiled down at her.

Misty did three more numbers, taking requests from the crowd. Their burgers came, and they took bites while enjoying the music. Misty finally stopped and headed over to the bar for a break with her mom.

"I could listen to her sing forever. She has such a lovely, throaty voice." Melody loved to sing herself, but not around people. Only alone. Her voice was certainly nothing like Misty's. "I'm glad you heard she was here this weekend and brought me."

"Glad you're enjoying yourself." He eyed her. "You are enjoying yourself, aren't you?"

"I am," she assured him. She was having a

great time. And he'd finally, *finally* asked her out again.

They sat through another set of Misty's songs, then Melody glanced at her watch. "I guess we should head out. It's getting kind of late and I have the early shift tomorrow at the cafe."

Ethan motioned for the server, paid the bill, and they headed across the restaurant.

"Thanks for coming," Willie called out from the bar area. "Come back soon."

Ethan waved. "We will."

The way he said *we* warmed her heart.

We. It was nice being part of a we.

The night air was cool, salty, and refreshing. Ethan took her hand in his. She rested her other hand on his arm as they walked down the sidewalk to his car. He might have brushed the tiniest of kisses against the side of her forehead. So light that she almost thought she imagined it. Had he kissed her? Maybe he'd just bumped into her slightly, leaning his head close.

When they got to his car, he opened the door for her. She slid inside and he went around to the driver's side and climbed in. They headed down Oak Street to the bridge and off the island.

The low light of the dashboard cast a warm, intimate glow around them. As they drove along the road back to Moonbeam, it was almost like it was just the two of them, alone in the world. Connected. Her heart was at peace for the first time in a very long time. Contented. Happy.

They rode along in the most comfortable silence she'd ever experienced. When they finally got back to her home, he opened the door for her and reached out a hand. She took his hand, and he helped her out of the car. For a moment, she stood almost right against him. He stepped back slightly and let her pass.

At the front door, she opened it a crack, then turned around, waiting. Waiting for his good-night kiss. For the kiss she'd been waiting for—for what seemed like a very, *very* long time.

He stood there for a moment. "Had a great time, Mel. Great time. Thanks for going with me."

"I had a lovely time, too." Still waiting…

He nodded. "Good night. I'll see you tomorrow. I'll be by for breakfast at the cafe." He turned and headed back to his car.

Her mouth dropped open. That was it? *Good night* was it? He pulled his car out, his lights dimming as he drove away. She slipped into her house.

What was wrong? Why didn't he kiss her? She touched her lips. The lips she'd been sure would be kissed tonight.

She *wanted* to be kissed tonight. Disappointment flowed through her. Just one little good-night kiss. Was that too much to ask?

"Ethan, you're driving me crazy," she muttered as she flicked on the light and strode across the room, her footsteps echoing on the wooden floorboards.

CHAPTER 19

J ack ran extra miles on Monday morning, hoping to chase away his thoughts. His confusion. His… pain. He could barely admit to himself that he'd fallen so hard for Daisy and so quickly. And then—poof—she was gone. She'd made it quite clear she wasn't interested in dating him.

He slowed down to begin cooling off.

But he just *knew* she felt something when they kissed. Knew it. His heart beat faster just thinking of those kisses.

Nope, he was supposed to be cooling off, not heating up. He slowed his pace even more, hoping that would help. He glanced up the beach and saw Rose sitting at her regular spot. Suddenly, he longed for a friend to talk to, and Rose was as close as he had at this point. She waved to him as he got closer and he jogged up to her, dropping down in the sand beside her.

"Didn't think I'd see you today. The sun's been up for a bit. Later than you usually run." Her eyes sparkled with warmth. A warmth that he needed today.

"I ran a few extra miles."

"Any reason?"

"I just... sometimes it helps when I'm... out of sorts."

"And what's got you out of sorts?" Her question was more caring than intruding.

"I..." A long sigh escaped him. "It's Daisy."

"You've been dating."

"We had one date. Things were going so well. At least I thought so. We were getting close. And I know she felt it, too. But then, suddenly, she just shut down. Decided she didn't want to date me. Told me to leave."

"I'm sorry. That must have been hard." Rose reached over and covered his hand. "Do you have any idea what happened?"

"No, not a clue. Even on a good day, I'm not

that great at figuring out women. But I just don't know what I did."

"Maybe it wasn't something you did. Maybe it's something about her."

"What do you mean?"

"Maybe getting close to someone was... scary for her. Maybe it's not the right time."

"Maybe." Disappointment shot through him. Maybe Rose was right. Daisy just wasn't ready to date.

"What happened when she changed her mind, do you know?"

"Nope. I just told her about my second job doing beach rescue. And she just kind of froze up." He shook his head. "And I was beginning to... to care about her. Have feelings for her. Even though I swore off dating women after the fiasco with Monique."

"I don't think you should swear off women after one bad relationship."

"I sure messed up my first attempt since Monique."

"Maybe you should try and talk to Daisy. Maybe it's something the two of you could work out."

"I don't know. She pretty much threw me

off her deck. Asked me to leave. It was a couple days ago and I haven't seen her since."

"Sometimes people need time to adjust to change. Maybe it was just a bit too fast for Daisy. You could talk to her. Maybe take things slowly. Maybe even just be friends for a bit. Give her time," Rose suggested.

"Maybe. But I'm not sure if she'd even talk to me."

"It's worth a try, isn't it?"

He pushed off the sand. "I'll think about it. Maybe I could try to talk to her."

Rose smiled. "I hope it works out."

He turned and jogged back home, wondering if Rose was right. Or what if he tried to talk to Daisy, and she shut him down? Again.

Daisy had been grateful to work alone on Sunday and not have to field any questions from Ellen. No such luck today, though.

"Daisy, you okay? You seem a bit out of sorts today."

"I'm fine. Just tired, I guess." But it was way more than just being tired.

"If you say so." Ellen's eyes said she didn't believe her. "Hey, do you have another date planned with Jack?"

"No, we decided that we weren't going to date." Well, *they* hadn't decided anything. *She'd* decided. But Ellen didn't need to know that.

Ellen's eyes widened in surprise. "Really? I thought you two were really getting along."

"I'm not really wanting to date now, anyway. The store keeps me really busy."

"But you need a life outside of work." Ellen's forehead wrinkled in concern.

"I've got plenty in my life. I love the shop. Love working with the flowers. It brings me joy. I have a really good life." She would just keep repeating that mantra.

"But—"

She held up a hand. "I don't really want to talk about it, okay?"

Ellen didn't look pleased, but nodded and turned back to work.

Daisy stayed at the shop after it closed, doing the extra bookwork she'd put off. Double-checking orders that didn't need double-checking. Her stomach growled, and she reluctantly locked the shop and headed for home.

As she got to her cottage, she saw light spilling out of Jack's windows, so he must be home. Too bad, because she wouldn't mind sitting outside with a cup of chamomile tea. But now she didn't want to take the chance that Jack would see her sitting out there. Maybe even come over and try to talk to her.

She slipped inside the front door and only turned on one lamp. Luckily, the kitchen was on the far side of the house from Jack's so she could at least turn on the under-cabinet lighting and he wouldn't know she was home. She made herself a sandwich in the dim light and put a kettle on for tea.

She sat at her kitchen table, alone, eating her meager meal and sipping her tea. Loneliness hovered around her. The severe kind of loneliness she'd had right after Kirk... was gone. How had she let herself get back into this kind of situation?

"Yes, I'm listening to you," she muttered to her smarter self. The self that had warned her not to fall for Jack. "I'll get over him. Soon. I promise." Her smarter self didn't seem to believe her.

CHAPTER 20

Daisy was pleased she hadn't seen Jack in five days. Or not pleased, depending on her mood. Jack's lights were off when she got home Thursday night after hiding out—no, *working* late. Okay, not really work that needed to be done, but work that kept her busy. Since Jack wasn't home, she decided to risk sitting out on her deck—though she still had the uncomfortable metal chairs. She hadn't had the energy to go shopping for something more comfortable. And besides that, she hadn't sat outside since the night she told Jack to leave.

And he'd left. And hadn't called, texted, or stopped by. She was grateful he'd taken the not-so-subtle hint. To just leave her alone.

And alone she was. A lonely alone too. With an empty house that mocked her without any personal touches to say it was home.

She poured herself a glass of merlot and snuck outside. Which was ridiculous if she thought about it. It was her deck. Her cottage. Her right to be outside. Still, she grabbed the solar lantern from the deck and shoved it inside. If she sat out here in the dark, even if he came home, he wouldn't see her.

She propped her feet up on an ottoman—also metal and hard—and took a sip of her drink. Her life had changed so much in the last few weeks. From the highs of dating Jack to the lows of being alone again. A feeling so familiar. One that she thought she'd gotten used to after Kirk's death. But she hadn't.

"Hey, Daisy. Can we talk?" Jack's voice came out of nowhere, but his shadowy figure rose up the deck stairs.

"Jack." Her heart did a triple beat at seeing him. A triple beat it wasn't supposed to do because she was concentrating on getting over him.

"If you want me to leave, I will. But I just really would like to talk."

But there wasn't much to say, was there? She couldn't date him. *Wouldn't* date him. "Jack, I'm sorry. There's really nothing to talk about. I'm just not ready to date anyone."

"Anyone? Or just me?"

She couldn't really see his face clearly in the darkness, but she could hear the hurt in his voice.

"Can you tell me why you changed your mind? I know you felt something, Daisy. I know you did. I wasn't imagining it."

No, he hadn't been imagining it.

"Please, just talk to me."

She realized she did owe him some kind of explanation. Not that she wanted to tell her story. But if she did, then maybe he'd understand. Maybe he'd leave her alone. Maybe he wouldn't feel hurt. She hadn't meant to hurt him. She just wanted to protect herself.

"Okay, sit down."

"Mind if I grab the lantern you hid inside so I wouldn't see you out here?" His voice hid a tinge of amusement.

She laughed gently in spite of herself. "Sure, it's right inside the door."

He grabbed the lantern and set it in front of

the chairs. She could see his face now. Confused. Serious. He settled in the chair next to her, sitting rigidly instead of his usual sprawl.

Silence fell between them while she tried to figure out how to explain everything. What to say. Dredge up the courage to tell him what happened. She hadn't told a single soul about it. Oh, everyone in Sweet River Falls knew what happened. She could see it in their faces when they ran into her. The pity. The quickly hidden look of relief that it hadn't happened to them. One of the reasons she'd fled Sweet River Falls.

He finally broke the silence. "Rose said I should come talk to you. That maybe we could work it out..." He looked over at her. "Can we work it out? Can we at least still be friends? I've missed you."

She'd missed him too, though she hadn't wanted to admit it. She took a deep breath, trying to find the strength to tell her story. To live through it again. "It's... it's me, not you. I just can't go out with someone with a dangerous job. It's too risky."

"My job is why you won't date me?" He furrowed his brow. "It's not really dangerous.

Well, I guess it can be at times. But mostly it's just routine."

"Until it isn't." She looked directly at him now. "You see... I was engaged. Engaged to Kirk. Engaged for seven days."

He searched her face but sat quietly and let her speak.

"Kirk was with the ski patrol. He loved it. Being outside. Skiing. Taking the snowmobiles up the mountains. Usually, it was just taking a skier who got injured back down the mountain. But the last time..." She paused, slowly stroking her hands along her thighs to loosen them from the fists she'd made. "There was an avalanche."

She closed her eyes against the memories, against the pain that was surging through her. The reason she never spoke of those horrible days.

She opened her eyes again. "After the avalanche, they went out to search for survivors. But there was still the threat of more avalanches. The mountain was closed. I begged him not to go. It was too dangerous. But... he went anyway."

Jack reached over and took one of her hands in his, still silently listening.

"About an hour or so after he left, I got a text warning about another avalanche. I went to the ski patrol base at the bottom of the mountain, desperate to hear some news about Kirk. See if he'd checked in. If he was okay." A lone tear trailed down her cheek. "But they hadn't heard from him. They couldn't pick up his transponder signal. I stayed there for two days. Waiting for word. Nothing."

"I'm so sorry." His words were full of sympathy, but she didn't want it. She couldn't bear to hear the sympathy in everyone's words.

"I finally went home and waited for news. But there was just no word. Until finally... they found his body."

She looked up defiantly. "And it wasn't the first time this has happened to me. My father was a police officer. He was killed in the line of duty. He was at a bank when a robbery occurred. He was locked inside with the robbers. Mom and I went over there when she heard about it on the police radio she listened to. We waited and waited. Then we heard gunshots. Dad never came out. That's when I first realized that I could never be with anyone who did a dangerous job." She took a shaky breath. "But then… Kirk won me over. Insisted nothing would ever happen to him. And I began to believe him. Enough that I finally said yes when he asked me to marry him. That was seven days before he died. Seven days."

Jack got out of his chair and knelt before her, holding both her hands now. "That must have been so hard on you. It's so tragic. And not only losing your dad but losing Kirk too. I'm sorry for your losses. I truly am. But I'm glad you told me what happened. Now I understand why you don't want to date me."

"I can't… I can't date you and risk going through that again."

He nodded. "I understand. And I'm sorry it worked out this way for us."

"I am too."

"So, do you think we could still be friends? Put the whole dating thing away? Just have fun together? I've missed talking with you. You make me laugh. I've just… missed you this week."

"I've missed you too. But I can't date you. You understand, right?" She searched his face.

He nodded. "I do understand. And I won't press you for a date again. We'll just step back.

Be friends. I can live with that." He looked into her eyes. "Can you?"

Could she? Was it even too risky to just be friends? But she had missed him. Talking to him. Laughing with him. She took a deep breath of the salty air and squeezed his hands. "Yes, let's go back to being friends. That will work." She hoped that would work…

He stood and looked down at her. "Good. I'd like that. And Daisy, I'm truly sorry you went through all of that. You're a strong woman. You moved on and opened your own successful business. Didn't let it crush you. I can't say I blame you for not wanting to date someone with a rescue job."

She stood up beside him. "I'm glad you understand. And I'm glad we talked. I didn't like how it ended between us."

"I didn't either. But we'll be okay now, won't we? Just friends."

"Just friends."

"And now you can quit hiding from me." His lips curled into a grin. "I should go now." He climbed down the stairs and turned back toward her. "Daisy… I'm really glad you told me what happened. And I'll see you soon."

With a wave, he jogged across the sand to his cottage.

She sat back on the metal chair, her heart racing. She'd finally told her story to someone. Someone who hadn't been there when it happened. A tiny bit of relief drifted through her for just sharing it with someone. With Jack. A man she'd come to trust. A man who she'd just be friends with now.

Jack trotted barefoot across the cool sand and slipped into his cottage. Finally, the mystery of why Daisy had pulled away from him was revealed. He couldn't blame her, either. Twice she'd lost people she loved to their jobs. That had to have been so tough on her.

He sank onto his couch, propping his feet on the coffee table. It was clear that Daisy wasn't going to change her mind about this. And that was okay. She had to do what she had to do to protect herself. He got that.

He briefly toyed with the idea of quitting the rescue unit even though he really enjoyed working with them. But they were short-staffed, and if he left, they'd be in even worse shape.

Maybe he could turn in his notice but wait until they found someone to replace him. That might work. Though it would probably take a while. They'd been looking for months for help before they hired him.

He leaned back on the couch, surprised he was even considering leaving a job he loved so much. But even though he'd only known Daisy for a few weeks, he'd fallen for her. Fallen hard. And at this point, he'd be willing to leave the job for a chance at dating her.

Wouldn't he?

He frowned in the darkness. But would that work? Would he end up resenting her for making him leave a job he enjoyed so much? He still had his regular job. One that paid him good money, unlike the rescue work. Rescue work was long hours and low pay. People did it because they enjoyed it. And there was something to be said about enjoying your job, no matter the pay.

So many questions and so much to think about.

Nothing was going to get decided tonight. He shoved off the couch and headed to bed.

The look on Daisy's face when she told him what happened haunted him. The pain. The sadness.

He could never be the one to put a look like that on her face. Ever.

CHAPTER 21

Aspen walked into the office at Jimmy's and Walker looked up from his desk, a quick smile coming to his lips. "Hey, beautiful."

Happiness swelled through her. "Hey, yourself." She walked over and perched on the side of his desk. "Thought I'd come say hi before my shift started."

Walker rose from his seat and came to stand in front of her, wrapping his arms around her and pulling her close to his chest. "I missed you."

"It was only one day." She laughed.

"An eternity." He kissed her forehead and stepped back. "We should give you shifts every single day."

She laughed. "Not sure how that would work out for Violet if I worked here every day. She needs me at the cottages too."

He let out an exaggerated sigh. "I know."

She grinned. "But we do have a date scheduled for Sunday."

"I know. Just you and me. No work. No other people. I can't wait." He took her hands in his and squeezed them.

"But you're trusting me to cook for you. Kind of risky."

"I'll take my chances. Besides, I'm bringing the steaks, and I know how to grill them."

"But you're depending on me for the rest of the food. I still say it's risky." She hadn't really ever had the need to cook much. Just make something quick for herself. Now she was going to try to pull off baking him a cake as a surprise. She hoped it turned out. It wasn't like her mother had ever taught her a thing about cooking. Or much else, for that matter. She shoved her memories of Magnolia away. Now was not the time to think of her mom.

"Anyway, for now, I have to get to work. My boss is quite the taskmaster." She tossed him a sassy grin.

"I've heard that about him. Not sure why you work for him." A smile played at his lips.

"Because I love him." She stood up on tiptoe and kissed those smiling lips.

"He loves you too." He pulled her back into his arms.

She stood there, enjoying being near him, feeling his heart beat against her cheek pressed to his chest. Enjoying their few moments alone.

Tara popped her head in the door. "Hey, we're starting to get busy. You two can't just stand in here all day kissing."

"Can too if I want to, sis," he retorted. "I'm the boss."

"Right, and I just let you keep believing that lie." Tara rolled her eyes at him.

"It's the truth. I'm older than you, so ergo, I'm the boss."

"Fifty-fifty split, old man. Half and half bosses." Tara shook her head and disappeared.

Aspen loved the way the two siblings teased each other and knew they adored each other. She laughed and pulled out of Walker's arms. "I've got to get to work."

"Walk you home after we close?"

"Sounds like a plan."

She headed out into the restaurant, tied on a server apron, and got to work. Daisy and Jack came in for a meal. The Jenkins twins had been by earlier this week, saying no one had seen them out together in a while. And here they were, together, proving the twins wrong.

The evening was busy, but she liked that. Tips were good tonight, too. The crowd finally died down, and she helped clear the last tables and carried the dishes into the kitchen.

Tara was in there tidying up. "Thanks." She took the tray of dishes. "Why don't you head home? And tell Walker I'll close up tonight."

"You sure?"

"I'm sure."

Aspen hung up her apron and headed to find Walker. She finally found him in the supply room. "Hey, Tara said she'd close up tonight."

He placed a box in a stack and turned to her. "Perfect. Then are you ready to go?"

"I am."

They headed out onto the wharf, hand in hand, strolling under the lights strung across between the shops. Most of the shops were closed now. Moonbeam wasn't a very active town late at night. But she loved that. Just a sleepy little town she adored.

"You look happy. Or maybe content," Walker said.

"I am. Very. I was just thinking about how happy I am that I came to Moonbeam."

"I'm happy you came here too." His warm eyes sparkled with love as he slipped his arm around her shoulders.

"Oh, and did I tell you? I talked to my sister. She's coming to stay at the cottages for Christmas. Willow, Derek, and Eli. I'm so excited. A real family Christmas. She said her son, Eli, is so excited about having Christmas at the beach."

"Knowing Mom, she'll probably insist that you bring them all over to her house for Christmas. You know how she loves to throw a big get-together."

"I'm really looking forward to Christmas this year. Usually, I'd just offer to work extra shifts for people who had kids."

"We're closed Christmas Day, and close early on Christmas Eve. My folks always say their workers should have the time to be with their families. Tara and I are keeping up the tradition."

Walker and his family really were the nicest people in the world. And his family had embraced her as one of their own. She felt like she finally had a family now.

He paused under a lamplight and turned her to face him. "My life has really changed since you moved here. For the better. I can't imagine my life without you in it. And I'm so glad you found out you had a sister, a family."

Happiness swelled through her again. She was happy. She had a newfound sister, Willow. Was hopelessly in love with Walker. Had a wonderful place to live at the cottages. Adored working for Violet. Had made so many friends here in Moonbeam, like Violet and Rose. She'd never had so much joy in her life.

She reached up and touched his cheek. "Walker, you are the best thing that ever happened to me."

He grinned at her. "Right back atcha." He covered her hand with his, and the warmth flowed through her.

They started down the sidewalk again, the stars twinkling above them, the night air cool against her skin. It was the most perfect night ever, as far as she was concerned. Perfect.

Okay, it might get a bit better when Willow came back to town. But it was sure pretty darn perfect now.

CHAPTER 22

Daisy was glad that she and Jack worked things out. He seemed fine with just being her friend. And that was all she had for him. Friendship. With time, she was certain she'd tamp down any other type of feeling she'd begun to feel toward him.

Just friends. That was her mantra every time she saw him. Like when they went out to Jimmy's to eat the other night. The twins had come by and insisted again that the two of them were dating. But Jack set them straight. Reiterated they were just friends. Although the twins didn't seem convinced.

But it was fun to hang out with Jack again.

The dinner at Jimmy's. Drinks on his deck one night.

Daisy hurried home from work about noon to wait for a delivery. And why was it that delivery people never could give you a very good estimate on time? They'd just said anytime this afternoon. Luckily Ellen could work the shop.

But she was excited about the delivery. Two wicker chairs with plump cushions and two ottomans for her deck. She also found a small table that she was going to place along one wall inside. Then she'd go out thrifting to find the perfect small items to place on it. She was surprised how much fun she was having shopping for all of this.

And since she was home for the afternoon, she decided to hang the two paintings she'd found at Bella's Vintage Shop over on Belle Island. One was a painting of two Adirondack chairs with a large-brimmed hat and a bright towel blowing in the wind. The waves curled in the background, and birds flew through the fluffy clouds. It was painted by a local artist from Belle Island, Charlotte Duncan. She adored it.

The other painting was of a blue heron,

painted on weathered boards. It was tall and narrow, and she had the perfect spot for it. She hung the blue heron painting but waited to hang the beach scene. She wanted to hang it over the table that was being delivered and wanted to get it in just the right spot.

The delivery men came and carted in the furniture and unpacked it. They put the wicker chairs and footrests out on the deck, and the table beside the wall, and hauled off the boxes.

She stood in the room, looking around. It was amazing how just a few touches made the place feel more like home. She couldn't wait to have Jack over and show him. Maybe she'd have him over for drinks this evening.

Out on the deck, she adjusted the chairs so they were both facing the water, a small distance apart. She'd have to use the small metal table for now, but she'd look for something different to go between the chairs. She carted the metal chairs to the garage, thinking she'd probably donate them to the thrift shop in town that benefited several local charities.

She got a glass of iced tea and went out to enjoy the chairs. The bright sunshine warmed her skin, and she put her feet up on the ottoman. Perfect. And ever so comfortable. She sipped on the tea until it was gone and set the glass of melting ice on the table. She closed her eyes for a moment, just enjoying the afternoon.

She woke up later with a start and looked at her watch. She'd slept for an hour. She never napped. She shook her head, clearing her thoughts, and stood. She glanced over at Jack's —strictly out of habit now—and saw him walking out onto his deck. She started to wave until a beautiful woman stepped outside right behind him. Jack stood with his back toward her, but she could see the woman clearly. She draped her hands around Jack's neck. Then she kissed him.

Daisy swallowed hard. It certainly hadn't taken him long to find someone new to date. She didn't know why that made her heart squeeze. Because she was the one who had made the rule that she wouldn't date him. *Couldn't* date him. She should be happy for him.

She grabbed the glass and twirled around, heading inside. Okay, so maybe she wouldn't invite Jack over tonight to see all the new furniture and have a drink out on the deck. Obviously he was busy.

And now she was stuck inside because she certainly didn't want to be out on her deck watching him kiss another woman.

Jack reached up and carefully pried Monique's hands from his neck and stepped back. "What are you doing?"

"Kissing you. It was nice, wasn't it?"

"Monique, you made it clear you wanted nothing to do with me when I moved to Moonbeam. Then you show up here unannounced."

"Oh, that was just a little spat. You knew I wasn't serious."

He eyed her. She'd certainly seemed serious enough when she broke up with him all those weeks ago. Even threw a vase at him, shattering it against the wall with flowers spilling everywhere. *That* seemed serious.

What was she doing here now?

"I figured I gave you a enough time to have a nice little visit with your mom. I'm sure you're ready to move back home by now, aren't you? There's just nothing to do in a town this size.

You can't possibly be happy here. Boston has everything. Sports. Theater. Fabulous restaurants."

"Monique, I'm not moving back. This is my home now. My mother needs me." Which wasn't really the truth because he'd come to realize his mother was definitely capable of taking care of herself. But he'd also realized he liked being here near her, near family.

"You don't mean that." Monique pouted. "I'm sure you could find someone to take care of your mom. It doesn't have to be you."

"But I like living here."

"That's silly. I mean, what in the world do you do for fun here?"

"Lots of things. Run. Go out to eat on the wharf. Swim in the sea. I've got friends here now. I'm happy here." And he had his rescue unit job. The one he still hadn't decided whether he was going to keep or not.

And he did have friends. Daisy was a friend. And Rose. She'd become a friend too.

"But there's more to do back in the city. And I'm back there."

"Monique, you're not listening to me." And he realized Monique had never listened to him.

Just always said what she wanted. And he'd usually given in. But he had no interest in that anymore. He loved his new life here in Moonbeam.

He walked back inside, and Monique followed. "But, Jack." She stood with her hands on her hips, pouting. "All your real friends are back home. Don't you miss them? Miss me? You want to come back home, don't you?" She tilted her head to the side and gave him what he was certain she thought was a beguiling look. He wasn't beguiled.

And, truth be told, he hadn't ever considered Boston home. Even though he'd lived there for six years. It never felt like home to him.

A quick triple knock sounded at the door, and he whirled around, already knowing who it was. The door swung open and his mom bustled in.

"Jackson, I was coming back from knitting club and thought I'd bring you this plate of—" His mom paused just inside the door, holding a plate of cookies. "Oh, I'm sorry. I didn't know you had company."

"No, Mom. That's okay. Come in." He

took the offered plate and glanced down. Chocolate chip with pecans. His favorite. Of course. He set them on a small table by the door.

"Aren't you going to introduce me?" His mom moved a few steps into the cottage.

Monique walked up to him and slipped her arm around him. "I'm Monique. Jack's girlfriend. You must be Mona."

His mom looked at him questioningly but smiled at Monique. "So nice to meet you."

"Jack and I were just discussing him moving back to Boston."

His mom's eyes widened. "Oh? I thought…" She shook her head. "Never mind. It's Jack's decision. I love having him here, but I just want him to be happy. I'm fine living here alone. I have lots of friends, and my villa's upkeep is all done for me. Jack is free to return to Boston, of course."

Monique smiled victoriously.

He slipped out of Monique's arm—which had tightened possessively around his waist— glared at her, and walked over to his mom. "Mom, I'm not leaving Moonbeam. I like it here."

"You're free to do what you want, son. I'll be fine."

He glanced over at Monique, whose cheeks held two bright dots of red. He knew what was coming. An explosion. She hated to be contradicted.

"Ah, Mom. Thanks for the cookies. You think you could give Monique and me some time?" Anything to get her out of here before Monique started yelling. Which he knew was coming.

"Yes, of course. I'm sorry to interrupt."

He kissed her cheek. "Mom, you're never interrupting. Always welcome here."

She turned and headed for the door with one last look at him, then Monique. He closed the door behind her and whirled around.

"What was all that? Why would you say that to her?"

"She was perfectly clear that she didn't need you here. You have no reason not to move back to Boston." Her eyes glittered in anger, demanding to have her way. Then, just as quickly, she turned all buttery sweet. "Come on. We'll have so much fun again. You said you loved me."

He knew one thing for certain. He'd *never* told Monique he loved her. Because he hadn't. He took a step toward Monique, her wheedling tone getting on his last nerve. "Let me make this perfectly clear. I am not moving back to Boston. I'm staying here. And there is no us. Not any longer. We're not dating. I'm not moving back. Is all that clear?" His words sounded harsher than he meant to say them, but Monique had to know he was serious. No moving back.

And just as quickly as she'd sweetened up, her face turned to fury, her eyes flashing. "Then don't you dare try calling me."

Her words rang across the room, echoing off the corners, the tone loud and furious. "And don't try to come back later. I'm through with you, Jack Rayburn. We're done."

She got dangerously close to the plate of cookies, and he hoped she didn't scoop them up and throw them at him. What a waste of cookies that would be.

She stalked past him, jerked open the door, and left, slamming the door behind her.

He stood staring at the door, feeling like a hurricane had just blitzed through the cottage. What had he ever seen in her? She was demanding and self-centered and just... annoying. And he was angry that she'd said all that to his mom. He should call his mom and straighten things out. Let her know that Monique was certainly not his girlfriend and he had no plans to leave.

He picked up the plate of cookies that thankfully hadn't been harmed in the storm that was Monique and took it to the kitchen. He snagged one and crunched on it. Even his favorite cookies did little to temper his annoyance.

Maybe he'd pop over to Daisy's and see if she wanted to sit out and have a drink. The evening was perfect weather for it. Though the weatherman said that a bad storm was headed their way in a few days. He laughed. A storm couldn't even compete with Monique. He craved Daisy's unflappable calmness and friendship. That would help. Then he'd call his mom and get that all sorted.

Daisy finished hanging the picture over the table and stood back to admire her handiwork. It looked perfect. The place was starting to come together and look like a home.

She heard a knock at the door to the deck and saw Jack standing there, smiling. *Wonder what happened to the gorgeous woman?* Not that it mattered to her, of course. She motioned for him to come in.

"Hey, Jack."

"I see you got new outdoor furniture. It looks great." He swung his glance around the room. "And look at this. New table. Pictures on the wall. Looking good."

"Thanks." She turned and straightened the picture on the wall, which was already perfectly straight, ignoring the pleased feeling flooding through her at his compliment.

"I was wondering if you want to have a drink. We could christen your new furniture."

"I, ah. No. I can't. I have to go back into work. I left early to wait for the furniture delivery, but I have things I need to do." Which was an outright lie, but it was for the best. He'd moved on to someone way more attractive than she was. And probably didn't have all the baggage she did. And, you know, actually *wanted* to date him. And that was fine. Just fine.

"Oh, that's too bad. Well, maybe tomorrow then." He gave her a friendly smile.

Which was the right thing to do because they were friends. Bet he didn't give that kind of smile to the beautiful one. He probably gave her that slow, sexy smile he used to give her. The one that had made her heart race.

"Ah, I'm working late tomorrow." That, at least, was the truth.

"Okay, well, soon then," he said cheerfully. He paused in the doorway and turned back to her. "You okay? You just seem... a bit... off?"

"I'm fine. Just busy."

He nodded. "Okay, good. I'll see you soon." He slipped out the door.

She turned back to the perfectly straight picture and sighed. Now she guessed she needed to head back to work since that's what she told Jack she was doing. At least then it wouldn't totally be a lie. And there *was* always work to be done at the shop. Feeling justified, she headed out the door to go back to the shop and do... *something*.

CHAPTER 23

M elody headed over to join Violet and Rose for coffee. Ethan had been in every day since their date but hadn't asked her out again. Nor had he kissed her any of the multiple times he'd walked her home after her shifts at the cafe.

She sank onto a chair next to Rose while Violet brought her a cup of coffee.

Violet handed her a welcome mug, and she blew on it, watching the steam dance.

"So what's new with you and Ethan?" Violet asked as she sat down in her chair.

"Nothing. Absolutely nothing. He hasn't asked me out again, though he does walk me home most evenings if I have the late shift at the cafe."

"But you had a good time on your date at The Lucky Duck?" Rose asked.

"A wonderful time." She sighed, glancing at her coffee, looking for answers before looking back up. "But I just don't get it. Why hasn't he asked me out again? And why…" The warmth of a blush rushed up her neck and covered her cheeks. "Why hasn't he kissed me again?"

"He hasn't?" Violet's eyebrows raised. "Hmm…"

"Hmm is right." She scowled. "I want him to kiss me."

"Maybe he's just taking things slow like you asked him to," Rose said.

"I know. But still… he can kiss me, can't he?" She set down her cup. "Maybe he doesn't want to. Maybe… maybe he's realized he doesn't like me that way. Just wants to be my friend."

Violet rolled her eyes. "Or maybe you're reading way too much into this. You could kiss him, you know."

"I know… it's just. I want him to kiss me."

"Maybe he's thinking the same thing. That he wants you to kiss him." Rose leaned forward. "Waiting for you to do it on your own time."

She frowned. "I never thought of that…"

"I bet Rose is right. He's waiting for you since you're the one who said you wanted to slow things down." Violet nodded vigorously, then grinned. "And Rose is usually right with her advice."

Rose laughed. "Not always."

"Usually pretty spot on," Violet insisted.

She chewed her lower lip. Maybe if Rose was right… Maybe he was waiting on her. If so, she'd wasted all this time. Because she sure did want to kiss him. She jumped up, swallowed the last of her coffee, and handed the cup to Violet. "I've got to run. Want to make sure I'm at the cafe in case Ethan comes in."

Violet smirked but didn't say anything.

"You have a good day, then." Rose nodded.

"I'm sure I will." She hurried down the steps and along the drive until she got to the sidewalk, walking at a brisk pace, a smile settling on her lips. A very good day.

Ethan finally came into Sea Glass Cafe toward the end of the lunch crowd. He took a table and waved to her. She finished up with her customer and hurried over to his table.

"Afternoon, Mel."

"Hey there." She nodded to him.

"What's the special today?"

So much sameness. Every single day. He comes in. He asks what the special is. He orders. Usually the special. She stared at him for a moment, exasperated. "Me." She pointed at herself.

"What?" He frowned.

"Me. I'm the special today." She reached down and took his hands, pulling him to his feet. "Me."

"I—"

"Ethan, I know I said we'd take it slow. We've talked about it. Talked about it too much, actually."

"It's okay. I get it. I'm fine with slow."

"I've been known to be wrong a time or two." She tilted her head, a smile playing at her lips.

He frowned. "Were you wrong this time? About what?"

"About everything. Going slow. Just… everything." She stood up on tiptoe, rested her hands on his shoulders, and kissed him lightly, feeling the shock surge through him. She pulled back and grinned, enjoying the surprised look on his face. So much so that she kissed him again, longer this time.

When she finally stepped back, his eyes widened as he glanced around the cafe. "Right here in front of everyone?" he whispered.

"Right here." She nodded. "Now, I'm going to go put your order in. You want the special. The lunch special." She started to walk away but paused and turned back to him. "Oh, and Ethan?"

"Yes?" He still looked shell-shocked.

"Next time *you* kiss *me*, okay?"

He broke into a wide grin. "You bet. I can do that."

"Soon?"

"How about when you bring that special back?"

"That would work for me." She headed into the kitchen, her heart fluttering, a silly smile on her face. That would work very nicely. Maybe she and Ethan were *finally* figuring out the dance.

CHAPTER 24

The storm crashed into Moonbeam as predicted a few days later. Daisy drove home from work in the downpour, then dashed into the house, shaking the rain from her hair and hanging up her coat when she got inside.

She flipped on a lamp to chase away the darkness, and the picture of the blue heron greeted her like an old friend. She walked over and ran her fingers along the weathered boards the artist had painted the heron on. "Hi there." Was she really talking to a painting? She was a nutcase. She smiled at the heron nonetheless.

A knock sounded at the door, and she hurried over to answer it. Jack stood outside, an umbrella in hand, holding a thermos. "I saw you come home. Thought you might like some hot chocolate to chase away the gloom of the storm."

She stared at him as he closed the umbrella and leaned it against the wall. She stood there on the rug, not moving, not asking him in. "Do you think that's a good idea?"

"I do. Why?" He frowned. "You busy?"

"It's not that… it's just…" She pushed her damp hair away from her forehead. "Are you sure your girlfriend won't mind? She's okay with you coming over and having a drink with me? Does she know we're just friends?" If the tables were reversed, she wasn't so sure she'd be okay with it. But of course, the tables weren't reversed. She wasn't Jack's girlfriend, just his friend.

His forehead creased. "My girlfriend?"

"I saw you. I know you've found someone to date. You kissed her."

"I don't know——"

"Jack, I saw you and her. Out on your deck the other day. It's okay. I want you to find someone to date. Someone who makes you happy."

He shook his head. She'd seen Monique. Annoyance swelled through him yet again.

"Daisy, you don't understand."

"No, it's okay." She still hadn't asked him in. "But this is probably not a good idea. I'm glad for you, though. I want you to be happy."

Daisy made him happy, he realized with a start. She's the one who made him happy. But if just being his friend was all he could get, he'd just have to be fine with that.

But he had to explain. "What you saw… For the record, Monique kissed me. But I didn't kiss her. She's my ex. She came to town to…" To stir up trouble, it appeared. "She wanted me to move back to Boston. To get back together."

"And are you considering that?"

"No, I'm not. Not at all."

"Why not?"

"Because I like it here in Moonbeam. There's my mom… and there's you." There, he'd said it.

"But I'm sure you have friends back there in Boston."

"Some. But definitely not Monique. She's

too toxic. I don't know why I dated her for so long. She's not my type. I don't think she even likes me very much."

"But that doesn't change things between us. We're just friends. That's all we can be."

He set the thermos on the ground and stepped forward, taking her hands in his. "But I want more than that."

"Jack, we've been through this. I just... can't." She snatched her hands away, a look of determination etched on her face.

"What if I told you I turned in my notice to the rescue unit? They've luckily already hired a new guy. He starts late next week. The timing was perfect."

She stared up into his eyes. "You'd do that?"

"Of course I would. I did."

"But you love that job."

He took a deep breath. "But... I love you more."

She stepped back, her hand at her heart. "What?"

"I said I loved you. And I do. I know it's only been a short time, but you absolutely enchant me. I love being with you. Talking to you. Spending time with you. And I want more than just being friends, Daisy. So much more."

"You love me?" Her eyes pierced his very soul.

"I love you, Daisy Compton."

"I. Oh. I…" She blinked up at him.

"So what do you say? Can we be more than friends?"

"You're sure about the job?"

"I'm positive."

She nodded slowly as a shy smile crossed her lips. "Yes, I think we could be more than friends."

Pure happiness swelled through him. "And do you think I could kiss you again?"

Now she was grinning. "Oh, I think that might be a brilliant idea."

He took her into his arms and kissed her gently, marveling at his luck. His luck to have Daisy in his arms, kissing her, holding her. She'd agreed to be more than friends.

He finally, and very reluctantly, pulled away. "Come on, let's have this hot chocolate."

They headed into the kitchen and she got out two mugs. He poured the hot chocolate, and they went to sit on the couch. He couldn't help himself. He kissed her again. She tasted of chocolate.

They sipped their chocolate and talked about everything and nothing as joy filled him. This was right where he wanted to be. Always. He kissed her again, just to prove his point.

His phone rang, and he set down his mug. "I should get that. Might be Mom."

Daisy nodded.

He slipped out the phone and frowned at the number. "Hello?"

"Jack. Thank goodness. We need you. We have a mayday coming in. Boat in trouble. A man and his two young daughters got caught out in this. Engine trouble. I'm short-staffed."

He looked over at Daisy, his heart breaking but knowing that he couldn't say no. "Be right there."

He clicked off his phone and turned to her. "I'm sorry. I have to go. They need me for..."

Her face froze, and she dropped her mug, spilling what was left of her drink on the wooden planks of the floor.

"There are kids out there. I... I have to go. You understand, don't you?"

"All too well." Her words were icy cold as she leaned down and sopped up the chocolate.

CHAPTER 25

S he sat back up and wadded up the napkin soaked in chocolate.

"I have to go. They need me." His eyes were so intense, pleading with her.

She would only ask one time. "Please, don't go. It's storming. It's too dangerous." *Is this really happening? Don't put me through this again!*

He stood up. "I'm sorry. I have to go."

His words echoed Kirk's.

"The new guy doesn't start until next week. We'll talk when I get back."

"No, we won't." Her heart pounded and her pulse skittered through her. "I can't..." The words were choking her. "I can't do this. I won't."

"I'm sorry. I have to do this." He strode across the room, gave her one last glance, and disappeared out the door.

Disappeared for the last time because they were over. Over for good this time. He'd just said he was finished with this job. That's why she'd kissed him. That's why she'd allowed her heart to melt. She thought being with him, caring about him, would be *safe*.

Yet, here she was. Stuck back in the same nightmare scenario. She got up and peered out the window. Flashes of lightning danced across the sky. The roar of the surf reached her all the way inside. She closed her eyes against the view, her heart crushing inside of her.

Lilac—genus *Syringa*, family Oleaceae. Tulip —genus *Tulipa*, family Liliaceae. Hibiscus— genus *Hibiscus*, family Malvaceae.

Nope, that wasn't working. Wasn't calming her down.

How cruel could life be? To keep putting her in this same position. Nothing could convince her to date someone who just jumped into danger. And Jack had chosen his job over her. Even knowing what she'd gone through with both her father and Kirk.

Hours ticked by as she sat on the couch, refusing to think about Jack out in the storm.

Yeah, right, her smarter self mocked her.

And where had her smarter self been tonight, anyway? Why had she taken this chance? He would always choose danger and rescue work over her. That's who he was. It was who Kirk was.

She sat alone in the dark as the hours crawled by. Waiting. But waiting for what? What Jack did and what happened to him was no longer her business. It was midnight when she heard a knock at the door. She slowly walked over, holding her breath, and opened the door.

Jack stood there, dripping wet.

Relief surged through her, but she hardened her heart against it.

"I wanted you to know I was okay. We got to them. Rescued the dad and his little girls. They're all safe at home now."

She nodded. She wasn't a monster. She was glad the family was safe. But that didn't change anything. He'd left to go out on a dangerous rescue. One day, he might not make it home.

"Can we talk?" He looked intently at her, his eyes pleading.

"No. There's nothing to say."

The sadness in his eyes tore at her heart, but she listened to her smarter self this time and ignored his eyes, his pain. "Good night." She closed the door and walked away. Away from Jack. Away from any opportunity for him to break her heart again—if her heart ever did become whole again, which she doubted.

CHAPTER 26

Daisy hadn't seen Jack in about a week, not that it helped much. Her heart was still crumbling in her chest, but she listened to every word her smarter self said to her.

Be strong. Don't think about him. You're doing the right thing. I said to stop thinking about him!

She threw herself into work, going in early and staying late until Ellen finally insisted she take a morning off. So today was that morning, and she didn't know what to do with herself. She'd had copious amounts of coffee, scrubbed the countertops, and mopped the kitchen floor. She tried to read, but her mind kept wandering. Wandering into dangerous territory. She dropped the book on the couch and pushed up.

Maybe a walk on the beach would help. She hadn't done that for a long time. She crept out onto the deck and peered over toward Jack's cottage. Good, he wasn't outside.

She padded down the stairs and headed off down the beach in the opposite direction of Jack's cottage. No use tempting fate. She walked for a long time, stopping occasionally to check out a shell that called to her, watching the gulls swoop overhead and the sandpipers race along the water's edge. It should soothe her. But at this point, she wasn't sure anything would comfort her.

Stop thinking about him!

She sighed and turned around to head home. Forget taking the morning off—she was going to head into work. She needed to keep busy.

The waves stomped their way in today as a westerly wind pushed them to shore. The white caps crested, folded over, and slid up the sand. Daisy shoved her hair back as the wind tossed it in her face. There was a yellow warning flag on the beach today, but she was pretty sure it would soon be a red flag.

She'd almost made it home when she caught

the sound of someone yelling and she stopped, looking around. There at the edge of the beach, a young girl stood dancing around, yelling, pointing. She ran over to the girl, who looked about twelve or so.

"What's wrong?"

The girl grabbed her arm and pointed out into the water. "My sister. She's out there. We were wading, and a wave caught her. Swept her out. Help her. I... I can't swim."

She spun toward the water and saw someone out past the cresting waves, a dot of bright orange, arms waving.

"I'm supposed to be watching her. She's only eight. The waves are taking her further and further away from me. It's a riptide. I know it. We learned about them in school." Tears poured down her cheeks as her words tumbled out. "Save her. Please."

Without thinking, she splashed out into the waves, turning sideways as a row of waves crashed into her, jumping over some swells, until she made it past the breaking waves. Soon, she realized she was stuck in the riptide, sucking her out to sea. At least it was taking her out toward the girl. Thankful for her years on the swim team growing up, she closed the distance between them.

She stretched her hand out, and the girl grabbed it. "It's okay. I've got you."

"I can't get back to the beach." Her words came out in gulps.

"You're okay. We're going to just float along now. We're in a riptide. We'll swim parallel to the beach until the riptide ends."

"I'm scared." The girl clung tighter.

"We'll be okay. Just hold onto my shoulders and I'll swim for us." At least she hoped they'd be okay. She wasn't sure how long she'd have to swim before the riptide ended.

The girl grabbed ahold of her shoulders, and she headed parallel to the beach with slow, even strokes, conserving her energy. She glanced over her shoulder at the girl. "What's your name, sweetie?"

"Matilda."

"Well, Matilda, just hang on and we'll ride this out."

"Okay. Don't let go of me."

"I won't. I promise. I've got you." She turned back to concentrate on her swimming. She could do this. She *had* to do this.

CHAPTER 27

Jack snatched his cell phone off the table when it rang, annoyed at the interruption of his workday. Or just annoyed at life in general these days since his world had exploded when Daisy had absolutely refused to talk to him. He'd left voicemail. He'd texted her. But absolute silence in return.

"Jack, we need you. There's a riptide out near you. Someone called it in. A little girl caught out in it. We're on our way. But can you check it out?"

He jumped up, shrugging off his t-shirt, then ran to the garage and grabbed the rescue buoy he kept hanging there. He turned and raced outside, heading across the beach. He saw a small crowd gathered at the shoreline and ran toward them.

A young girl was crying while an older couple tried to comfort her. "Are you a lifeguard?" The girl pointed to his buoy.

"Yes."

"My sister. She's out there. A big wave took her way out there. The lady from the flower shop is trying to save her."

His heart lurched in his chest, and he strained to see them. Any sign of them. Nothing. "Daisy?"

The girl nodded.

Daisy was out there? Where?

"Did you see which way they went?"

The man pointed down the beach. "That way. They were pretty far out. I called it in to the rescue unit."

He spun in the sand and sped off down the beach in the direction the man pointed, searching the water past the breaking waves. How long had Daisy been out there? Had she found the girl? His lungs begged him for air, but he didn't stop, didn't slow down. Fear surged through him. A fear like he'd never felt before.

Daisy was in danger. What was she thinking

going out during a riptide? Putting herself in danger like that?

The irony of that thought wasn't lost on him.

He continued his sprint until he finally caught sight of what looked like two people in the water, just offshore. Was it Daisy?

He continued to run and as he got closer, he realized with relief that it was Daisy, and she had a young girl in her arms as she waded toward shore. She was waist-deep and almost to shore when he reached them.

He plunged the few strides it took to reach them and took the girl from her arms. "You're okay?"

Daisy nodded. "Tired."

He reached out and grabbed her elbow, steadying her, as the three of them splashed through the shallow waves at the edge of the shore. What he really wanted to do was take her in his arms and never let go.

As soon as they exited the waves, Daisy dropped down onto the sand. He set the girl beside her and carefully assessed them both.

"You okay, Matilda?" Daisy asked.

"I'm okay." The girl gulped back tears. "My mom is going to kill me, though."

Daisy hugged her. "I think your mom is just going to be so glad to see you're okay."

"You shouldn't play in the waves when there are riptide warnings." He frowned at the girl, and she looked like she might break into tears.

Daisy glared at him. "You can teach water safety later." She pulled the girl up next to her and stroked her hair. "It will be okay. You're okay."

"Matilda." The older sister and a woman came running across the beach, calling out.

"Momma." Matilda jumped up and headed toward the woman, who scooped her up in her arms and kissed her repeatedly.

The woman put Matilda down, holding firmly to her hand, and headed back toward them, both daughters at her side.

Daisy struggled to get up, and he reached a hand down and helped her to her feet.

The woman reached them and threw her arms around Daisy, hugging her. "Oh, thank you. Thank you."

Daisy hugged her back. "I'm just glad I could get to her."

"You risked your life in that riptide."

"I couldn't just let her be all alone out there struggling to get to shore."

"I'll never be able to repay you." Tears rolled down the woman's cheeks.

"Thank you." The older sister hugged her too. "I shouldn't have let her get so close to the waves. We were just supposed to be shelling on the beach."

"She's fine now."

"You need to watch the flags on the beach. If there's a yellow or a red flag, stay away from the water." He couldn't help himself. This time, Daisy didn't glare at him. She nodded in agreement.

He wasn't sure his heart was ever going to stop pounding. He wanted to gather Daisy up in his arms and hold her until eternity.

He turned to her. "And what were you thinking? You should have called for help. Gotten a lifeguard or the rescue team out here."

"There wasn't time." Daisy eyed him defiantly.

"Thank you again," the mom said, wrapping her arms around each of the girls. "I better get Matilda back home. She looks exhausted."

The trio headed off and Daisy stood at his side, watching them walk away. He turned to her. "You want me to go back and get the car? I could pick you up. You looked tired."

"No, I'm fine."

He nodded. "Okay, then I'll walk you home."

To his amazement, she didn't argue with him. They trudged back to their cottages in silence. He wanted to offer to get the car again but didn't dare. When Daisy made up her mind, there was no talking her out of it. He knew that well enough.

He walked her to her cottage, and she gradually climbed the steps of her deck, one by one. He stood in the sand, watching her. She stopped at her door and turned to look at him.

"Daisy, you scared me half to death."

She raised an eyebrow.

He let out a long sigh and climbed the stairs, standing right in front of her. "I know, I know. It's how you feel when I go out on a rescue. I get it now. And I'm done with it. The new guy starts tomorrow."

"Unless they call you for an emergency." She eyed him.

"They won't after I'm off the unit. But I would have gone in after that girl today, just like you. If I can help someone, I'm always going to do it."

She slumped against the doorframe. "I know you would. Just like I couldn't stop myself even though I knew the conditions were bad. I couldn't just leave her out there. I'm a strong swimmer. I thought I could help. But I have to admit I was questioning my decision after a bit. But finally the riptide dropped us off and I could get us to shore."

He reached out a hand and brushed back a lock of her damp hair. "I'm so grateful you're okay."

She grabbed his hand as he pulled it back. "I was grateful to see you standing there when I got to shore. At one point out there, I wasn't sure we'd make it. And all I could think about was... you."

"Ah, Daisy." He pulled her into his arms, and once again she surprised him by not pulling away.

He finally let her go—reluctantly—and

stepped back. "I should let you go inside and get cleaned up. You're probably exhausted."

"I am." She nodded. "I think I'm even going to do the unimaginable and call Ellen and tell her I'm not coming in today. Tell her to close up the shop early."

"Really?" He eyed her skeptically.

"Really." She reached out and took his hand again. "Do you think you could come over this evening? I think... I think we should talk."

"Of course." His pulse quickened with hope.

"I need some time first. And a shower to get this sand off of me. And probably a nap." Her lips curved up in a small smile. "But come over about five?"

"I'll be here."

"Good." She disappeared inside.

His heart soared—tentatively—as he jogged back to his cottage. Tonight they'd talk. He pinned all his hopes on that talk.

But he just wasn't sure it was going to turn out the way he wanted it to.

CHAPTER 28

Daisy stepped into the shower, letting the warm water wash away the salt water and sand. She shampooed her hair—twice—before it felt like all the grit was out of it. Then, with the warm water pouring over her, she gave in to the urge for tears. They mixed with the shower water and she let them flow.

She'd been so frightened out there. Afraid she couldn't save Matilda, or herself. So many thoughts had raced through her mind. Kirk. Jack. Memories of Sweet River Falls. Then she'd tried to push them away and concentrate on her swimming. Counting the strokes. Slow, measured strokes. But each stroke seemed to call out Jack, Jack, Jack.

When her tears finally subsided, she shut off the shower, stepped out, and grabbed her towel. Wrapping it around her, she walked over to the mirror and brushed the steam off of it.

A bedraggled-looking woman stared back at her. And yet, there was something in her eyes. A spark of hope.

Today had given her a different perspective on Jack's and Kirk's lives. There was no way she could have *not* helped Matilda. But still, it didn't lessen the stress of waiting for someone to return... or not return.

Be careful. You're going to do it again. Forget Jack.

"Oh, be quiet," she chastised her smarter self.

Was her smarter self really smarter?

Or was she a coward? Unable and unwilling to take a risk for love?

She pulled on an old t-shirt and crawled into bed, exhausted, and let sleep comfort her.

CHAPTER 29

At four-forty-five Daisy still wasn't certain what she was going to say to Jack. She paced the floor, straightened the blue heron picture—twice—and precisely adjusted the stack of books on the coffee table. She had cold beer in the fridge, a bottle of red wine open and breathing, and a large pitcher of sweet tea, uncertain what Jack might want.

But none of that helped. She still didn't know what she was going to say.

Just as the clock proclaimed it was five o'clock, she heard the knock at the deck door. Her heartbeat quickened as she walked over and opened it. "Jack." The sunlight spilled around him. His hair was damp from a shower, his cheeks ruddy from his hours in the sun and salt air. He looked impossibly handsome. And... a bit scared?

"Hi." There was a tentative note to his voice that made it almost more of a question than a greeting.

"Come in. What would you like to drink?" She turned and headed to the kitchen, her heart skipping and her breath a bit ragged.

"Beer is fine."

She grabbed two from the fridge, popped off the caps, and handed him one. "Outside? We can enjoy my new furniture."

He just nodded and followed her onto the deck. She sank into one chair, and he took the other one. For a brief moment she wished she would have thought to get a loveseat. But they sat there separately, silently, sipping their beer. It was Jack who finally broke the silence.

"You wanted to talk?" He was braver than she was.

"I did. Do. I just... I'm not sure what I want to say."

"Say anything you want to say to me. Anything."

She took a deep breath. "I'm confused.

About everything. And I hate that feeling. I need… control."

He nodded. "I get that."

"I need to not be worried every time you leave for your work."

"I understand that more now than before. I was about to go crazy when I heard you'd headed out in that surf to rescue Matilda. Putting yourself at risk like that. I wasn't sure if… if you'd make it. I couldn't breathe. It was terrible."

"It is terrible. And I really don't think I can go through it week after week."

"I get that now. I do. And I'm serious about quitting the unit. I couldn't put you through that every time I went out. I don't want to put you through that. I want… I want to make you happy, Daisy."

"You don't think they'll call you in emergencies?"

"Nope. They play by the rules, and I wouldn't be covered by their insurance. If I ever saw someone in trouble, though, I'd still help. It's just who I am."

She nodded. "I get that. I would, too." She gave him a wry grin. "Obviously."

"You should have called for help," he said
sternly.

"Maybe. But she was so scared, waving her
arms. I didn't know how much longer she would
last. I'm a strong swimmer. I thought—hoped—
I could get there and save her."

He set down his beer and took her hand.
"I'm just so grateful you're okay."

"And I understand better how you and Kirk
—and my dad—had to do what you do. The
need to help people. The pull." She looked deep
into his eyes. "And I don't want you to resent me
for making you quit your job. So…" She got
ready to take the biggest risk of her life…

*Don't say it! Don't. Just walk away from him.
Forget him. He'll break your heart.*

She ignored her smarter self, who she was
now certain was just a more timid version, a
fraidy-cat version of herself.

"If you want to still work the unit, I'm okay
with that."

His eyes widened. "You would be okay with
that?"

"I would."

He shook his head. "No, I'm not going back
to that job. I can't put you through that every

256

week." Then he grinned at her. "And besides that, I have a selfish reason for not going back. Not working every weekend."

"And what's that?"

"I want to spend more time with you. That is… if you've decided we can try this again."

She squeezed his hand. "I would like that. Try again. See what happens."

A grin spread across his face from ear to ear. "You would?"

"I would. But there's one other thing you should know."

The grin deflated, and he eyed her cautiously. "And what's that?"

She took her hand from his and reached up to touch his face. "You should know that I love you."

He jumped up, pulling her with him, and let out a whoop. "Best thing I've heard in… well, in forever." He twirled her around on the deck.

She laughed out loud. "Jack, put me down."

He grinned and set her down. "Good idea, because I can't kiss you while I'm twirling you in circles."

"Then it's a good thing you've put me down. Because I'm ready for you to kiss me." It felt like she'd been waiting forever to feel his kisses again.

Watch it. He's going to break—

No, he's not. She chased her other self far away, ready to take back control. Make her own decision.

"Daisy? You there? You looked like you were far away for a moment."

She smiled up at him. "No, I'm right here. I'm right where I want to be. I'm just waiting for that kiss you promised me."

"And I always keep my promises." He leaned down and kissed her gently, a sigh escaping him as if he'd gotten everything he'd ever wanted.

She'd gotten what she wanted too. And she was no longer going to hide from life, afraid of getting hurt.

He pulled back slightly. "Hey, Daisy, can you say it again?"

She grinned up at him, lost in his eyes, his smile. "I love you, Jack." And she stood on tiptoes to kiss him again to prove her point.

CHAPTER 30

R ose sat out on the beach a few nights later, enjoying the sunset. Her last night here at the cottages. Sadness hovered around her, but she knew it was time. She had to go back home. She couldn't hide out here in Moonbeam forever. The house back home was sitting empty. There were things that needed to be done. It was time.

When she told Violet she was leaving, Violet made her promise she'd come back for Christmas. So she'd reserved her same cottage for two weeks during the holidays. Then she'd have some decisions to make.

"Hey, Rose." Jack's voice pulled her from

her thoughts. She smiled when she saw Daisy with him, holding his hand.

"Hi, you two." Perfect. They'd worked out their difference. That was wonderful.

"I heard you're leaving," Daisy said.

"I am. It's time. I have to get back home."

"I'm going to miss our morning talks when I'm out on my runs." Jack smiled at her. "And your advice."

"I'll miss you too." But she smiled brightly up at him, not wanting either of them to see her sadness. "But I'll be back for the holidays. I'll see you both then."

"Oh, are you going to be back in time for the Christmas gala at Cabot Hotel?"

"I am."

"I hear it's wonderful and they raise so much money for the local charities. It's all fancy dress. I'm going to have to find one." Daisy looked at Jack, her eyes shining and full of love. "I've got a handsome date for it."

Jack laughed. "And I'll have the most beautiful woman in the room on my arm." He glanced at her. "No offense, Rose."

She smiled. "None taken."

"We'll see you when you get back to Moonbeam, then," Daisy said.

"You sure will."

The two of them walked down to the water's edge, heading back toward their cottages. They stopped by the waves, and Jack pulled Daisy into his arms and kissed her.

Rose could hear Daisy's laughter across the distance. Such a great couple. She was pleased they'd worked things out. Sometimes it just took time and talk.

Although, sometimes time didn't fix things. It hadn't with her and her sister. But that was something to think about at another time. She sighed as she got up off the beach and brushed the sand off. She'd miss these times out on the beach. Feeling so connected to the world out here in nature. The salty air, the waves, the birds overhead. This place filled her soul with happiness and contentment.

She turned to head back to her beloved peach-colored cottage. She'd miss it while she was back home. But she'd be back soon enough. She had Christmas to look forward to now. And spending Christmas in Moonbeam with friends sounded way more appealing than spending it back home, alone in her house.

She gave one last look at the sea. "Emmett, I'm headed home. I have decisions to make. I hope I make the right ones."

I hope you enjoyed this book. What's up next? Well, it's Christmastime in Moonbeam. So much happens during the holiday season at Blue Heron Cottages. Secrets, surprises, and lots of holiday fun. Check out Christmas by the Bay, book seven in the Blue Heron Cottages series.

And, of course, we'll have Rose's book next. We can't forget about Rose! I can't wait for you to read it.

As always, I truly appreciate all of my readers. I hope you're enjoying this series as much as I'm enjoying writing it.

ALSO BY KAY CORRELL

COMFORT CROSSING ~ THE SERIES

The Shop on Main - Book One

The Memory Box - Book Two

The Christmas Cottage - A Holiday Novella (Book 2.5)

The Letter - Book Three

The Christmas Scarf - A Holiday Novella (Book 3.5)

The Magnolia Cafe - Book Four

The Unexpected Wedding - Book Five

The Wedding in the Grove (crossover short story between series - Josephine and Paul from The Letter.)

LIGHTHOUSE POINT ~ THE SERIES

Wish Upon a Shell - Book One

Wedding on the Beach - Book Two

Love at the Lighthouse - Book Three

Cottage near the Point - Book Four

Return to the Island - Book Five

Bungalow by the Bay - Book Six

Christmas Comes to Lighthouse Point - Book Seven

CHARMING INN ~ Return to Lighthouse Point

One Simple Wish - Book One

Two of a Kind - Book Two

Three Little Things - Book Three

Four Short Weeks - Book Four

Five Years or So - Book Five

Six Hours Away - Book Six

Charming Christmas - Book Seven

SWEET RIVER ~ THE SERIES

A Dream to Believe in - Book One

A Memory to Cherish - Book Two

A Song to Remember - Book Three

A Time to Forgive - Book Four

A Summer of Secrets - Book Five

A Moment in the Moonlight - Book Six

MOONBEAM BAY ~ THE SERIES

The Parker Women - Book One

The Parker Cafe - Book Two

A Heather Parker Original - Book Three

The Parker Family Secret - Book Four

Grace Parker's Peach Pie - Book Five

The Perks of Being a Parker - Book Six

BLUE HERON COTTAGES ~ THE SERIES

Memories of the Beach - Book One

Walks along the Shore - Book Two

Bookshop near the Coast - Book Three

Restaurant on the Wharf - Book Four

Lilacs by the Sea - Book Five

Flower Shop on Magnolia - Book Six

Christmas by the Bay - Book Seven

Plus more to come!

WIND CHIME BEACH ~ A stand-alone novel

INDIGO BAY ~

Sweet Days by the Bay - Kay's complete collection
of stories in the Indigo Bay series

ABOUT THE AUTHOR

Kay Correll is a USA Today bestselling author of sweet, heartwarming stories that are a cross between women's fiction and contemporary romance. She is known for her charming small towns, quirky townsfolk, and the enduring strong friendships between the women in her books.

Kay splits her time between the southwest coast of Florida and the Midwest of the U.S. and can often be found out and about with her camera, taking a myriad of photographs, often incorporating them into her book covers. When not lost in her writing or photography, she can be found spending time with her ever-supportive husband, knitting, or playing with her puppies - a cavalier who is too cute for his own good and a naughty but adorable Australian shepherd. Their five boys are all grown now and while she misses the rowdy boy-noise chaos, she is thoroughly enjoying her empty nest years.

Learn more about Kay and her books at kaycorrell.com

While you're there, sign up for her newsletter to hear about new releases, sales, and giveaways.

WHERE TO FIND ME:
My shop: shop.kaycorrell.com
My author website: kaycorrell.com
authorcontact@kaycorrell.com

Join my Facebook Reader Group. We have lots of fun and you'll hear about sales and new releases first!
www.facebook.com/groups/KayCorrell/

I love to hear from my readers. Feel free to contact me at authorcontact@kaycorrell.com

facebook.com/KayCorrellAuthor

instagram.com/kaycorrell

pinterest.com/kaycorrellauthor

amazon.com/author/kaycorrell

bookbub.com/authors/kay-correll